PUFFIN

Wrec

Robert Swindells left school at the age of fifteen and joined the Royal Air Force at seventeen-and-a-half. After his discharge, he worked at a variety of jobs before training and working as a teacher. He is now a full-time writer and lives with his wife, Brenda, on the Yorkshire moors. Robert Swindells has written many books for young people, and in 1984 was the winner of the Children's Book Award and the Other Award for his novel *Brother in the Land*. He won the Children's Book Award for a second time in 1990 with *Room 13*, and in 1994 *Stone Cold* won the Carnegie Medal and the Sheffield Book Award.

ROBERT SWINDELLS

WRECKED

PUFFIN BOOKS

*I wish to thank young clubbers Penny Luithlen and
Bali Rai who brought me up to speed*

PUFFIN BOOKS

Published by the Penguin Group
Penguin Books Ltd, 80 Strand, London, WC2R ORL, England
Penguin Putnam Inc., 375 Hudson Street, New York, New York 10014, USA
Penguin Books Australia Ltd, 250 Camberwell Road, Camberwell, Victoria 3124, Australia
Penguin Books Canada Ltd, 10 Alcorn Avenue, Toron to, Ontario, Canada M4V 3B2
Penguin Books India (P) Ltd, 11 Community Centre, Panchsheel Park,
New Delhi – 110 017, India
Penguin Books (NZ) Ltd, Cnr Rosedale and Airborne Roads, Albany, Auckland, New Zealand
Penguin Books (South Africa) (Pty) Ltd, 24 Sturdee Avenue, Rosebank 2196, South Africa

On the World Wide Web at: www.penguin.com

Penguin Books Ltd, Registered Offices: 80 Strand, London WC2R ORL, England

First published 2001
1

The moral right of the author has been asserted

Set in 13/15 pt Monotype Bembo
Typeset by Rowland Phototypesetting Ltd, Bury St Edmunds, Suffolk
Made and printed in England by Clays Ltd, St Ives plc

British Library Cataloguing in Publication Data

A CIP catalogue record for this book is available from the British Library

ISBN 0–141–31035–9

One

One in the morning. Up an alley at the side of a gutted shop a roll of carpet lies in a skip. Inside the carpet like a sausage in a sausage roll sleeps Yomper. As he sleeps he dreams. It's the usual dream, the one that gets him twitching and muttering. Now and then he'll cry out, but the cider fumes keep him from waking. This is Yomper's dream.

It's 6 June 1982 at Bluff Cove in the Falklands. He's nineteen, a para. Moving up under fire he's got separated somehow from his unit. Soggy peat underfoot and smoke like the moors on fire at home. He's a trained soldier but this is his first action and he's confused. In training they tell you what your objective is and how you'll attain it and away you go and it works. You're a team, see, you and your mates. Paras. Simply the best. You never look round and find there's you and no bogger else like now, and you don't get lost either. You always know where you're going, and if you don't there's a sergeant who'll tell you pretty damn quick.

He stops to peer through the drizzle, hoping to locate his mates. Right now one mate would do. Rattle of small-arms fire punctuated by flat detonations. Movement on his right, three guys . . . shit! *Throws himself flat, soaks up freezing water like a sponge. Three Argies, coming straight at him. No, four. Four of the boggers. It feels unreal, like he's in a movie.* A year ago I was mopping tables in a burger bar, couldn't even have told you where the flipping Falklands *were* but here I am and I don't half wish I wasn't. *He sticks out his right leg for stability, sights along the short barrel of his a.r. and notices something. They're not armed. That first one's got his hands up. The boggers're surrendering.*

Relief, then exultation. He rises to his knees and stands, keeping them covered, picturing himself marching these four tossers into HQ at gunpoint like flipping Rambo. Cheers from his mates. Maybe a medal, later. Dad'd like that. *He's forgotten momentarily that he has no idea where HQ is.*

They're walking straight towards him with their hands up looking hungry, half-frozen. They're his own age or younger. In another world they'd be strobe-lit faces down the club. Their leader's a corporal. He says something in Spanish. They all look apprehensive. When they're five metres from him the para barks, 'Halt!' Maybe they have a bit of English or maybe it's his tone. Anyway they stop, and it's then it strikes him he hasn't a clue what he's supposed to do with them. They're gazing at him, this Brit who holds their lives in his hands. Awaiting his order. What if they suss I'm bloody lost?

The small-arms fire seems to have intensified. He can't tell whether any of it's coming this way but he has to do something. He's noticed a rock outcrop nearby and gestures with his weapon for the Argentinians to take cover behind it. They comply with alacrity, losing some of their wariness at this indication of his intention to keep them alive. He joins them, wondering what the heck he's going to do next.

Abruptly the decision passes out of his hands. A sergeant comes thudding up, squats panting at his side, gasps 'What's your bloody game then, lad — desertion in the face of the enemy, is it?' Welsh accent.

'No, Sarge, I got separated from my unit, then . . .' He gestures towards his prisoners.

'Shoot 'em, dickhead.'

'Can't do that, Sarge, they've surrendered.'

'Ha!' The sergeant pivots on a boot heel, points his weapon at the Argentinians. It's only a split second, but their faces show they've time to know what's coming. The lad's impulse is to knock the barrel aside, but months of training shackle him and he watches, horrified, as the sergeant squeezes the trigger and the four boys jump, then crumple. The sergeant stands, gazes down at him. 'Now they've surrendered, lad. Come on.'

In his roll of carpet Yomper sobs, turns over, sleeps. Somewhere a clock strikes the quarter.

Two

'Where you going, our Dennis?'

'Out.'

'I know you're going out, I said *where*.'

'Nowhere, Mam.'

'How can you be going *nowhere*, you daft beggar?'

'Town, if you must know. Meeting my mates.'

'Oh aye. And what *mates* might these be, then?'

'What *mates*? Tim and Michael, of course. I don't *have* any other mates.'

'So who were the four men Teresa Summerscales saw you talking to in Market Square on Tuesday?'

'Four men, *what* four men?'

'*I* don't know, our Dennis, you tell me. Tramps, she said they were. Down-and-outs, sitting on a wall.'

'Oh, *them*. I wasn't talking to them, Mam, except in passing. They're drunks. The Midborough Wine Circle, they're known as. It's a joke.'

'A joke, is it? Four zombies who could have been men, sitting on a wall. Poor sort of joke, lad. The sort your dad thought was funny till I got fed up to the back teeth of him rolling in here stinking of booze and kicked him out. I hope you're not heading the same way, our Dennis, 'cause —'

'I'm *not,* Mam, course I'm not. Just because I said hello to a bunch of —'

''Cause I haven't worked my fingers to the bone keeping a decent home together, giving you the opportunity to get some qualifications and go to university, just so you can chuck it all away.'

'I *know,* Mam, don't worry. Everything's under control. My results'll be out next week, then you'll see.'

'Oh I'll *see*, will I? Only I'll tell you something I *didn't* see, our Dennis. I didn't see you doing a lot of revision back in June when they gave you all that free time.'

'*Ma*-am . . . I've told you a zillion times, I revised over at Michael's place 'cause it's quieter. You *know* what it's like here with our Jimmy and Marie screaming round all the time. Same at Tim's, so we used Michael's.'

'Aye, well I hope you're not lying to me, lad, 'cause that's the other thing your dad was good at. Lying. He was that straight-faced with it, I could never tell what was true and what wasn't. I don't think *he* could in the end.'

'Yeah, well *relax,* Mam, OK, and I'll catch you later.'

'Don't –'

'*Later,* Mam.'

Three

Brasso is not too drunk to notice the woman coming. He's forever on the lookout for the mother who abandoned him as a baby in a ladies' lavatory and this one seems the right age, and she's dangling a Yourprice carrier like the one he was wearing when the cleaner found him. Just before she draws level, the woman notices Brasso and makes a minor course correction so she won't pass too close to the low wall he's sitting on. Most people do that when they see Brasso. Cow nudges him. 'She's on to you, man, look at her spurt.' Yomper and Digby get back from a fraternal pee behind the berberis in time to see the fun.

'Oi, Missus.' Brasso's call makes the woman lower her head and hurry by, staring at the pavement. Brasso gets up, sets his bottle in its crumpled bag carefully on the wall and shuffles after her, shouting in his phlegm-rattly voice, 'Ever in Brum, love, ladies' lav, nineteen eighty-one?' She glances back, breaks into an ungainly trot and bursts through the swing doors of M&S like a spooked heifer. Brasso stops, stares at the doors for a bit, then turns and shuffles back, mumbling to himself.

'Fancied you, that one,' cackles Digby. 'Tell by the way she hung around.'

'Shut your gob, Digby.'

'No, she did, Brasso my son.' This from Yomper. Brasso glowers.

'I'm not your son, you cockney git. I've told you before, you've only one act of procreation in you and it's holding you together.'

Cow frowns. 'Act of what you say? You swallow a dictionary or somethin'?'

'Shurrup, Cow – get back in that woodpile.'

'Oooh, that racist talk.' Cow appeals to the other two. 'D'you hear what him say to me, guys?'

Yomper shakes his head. 'Didn't hear a thing. D'you, Digby?'

'Naw. Listen: what say we go down the supermarket, tap the punters? I'm thirsty.'

Yomper shakes his head. 'No need, look.' He nods towards the clock on the jeweller's shop. 'Ten forty-five: kids'll be here in a bit wanting a few cans. They'll give us more for doing the Thresher bit than we'd get in an hour, tapping.'

Digby pulls a face. 'Think they'll come, do you?'

'Course they will, don't they always?' He smiles. 'I reckon that Dennis is damn near as big a piss-artist as anyone here and he's what . . . sixteen?'

'Yeah.' Brasso nods. 'Sixteen. Late starter, I call that.' He snorts. 'Twelve, I started. Friggin' twelve.'

'Yeah but like, he's from a decent home and you're from a ladies' lavatory.'

The other three laugh. Brasso doesn't join in.

Four

'Dennis, my man.' Michael, leaning beside two slots in the post office wall. First Class and Overseas. Second Class. Dennis thumped him in the arm. 'Should be a label on your gob, Michael. *Lager*, it should say.' He laughed. 'First Class and Overseas, Second Class, Lager. All you'd have to do is stand there all day with it open and folks'd come and post cans. They'd fit sideways and all.'

Michael nodded. 'You're a devil–may–care jokester, Dennis. Where's the other clown?'

'Tim? He'll be along pretty soon.'

'Yeah, pretty soon compared to the history of the universe. I'm thirsty.'

Dennis nodded. 'You're not alone.'

'We'll give him a minute,' growled Michael, 'then head for Market Square.'

'Right. Have to watch it though.'

'How d'you mean, *watch* it?' Michael laughed. 'Sip it, sup it, slurp it; the three esses. Bogger watching it.'

'No, straight up. Some old tart saw us with the Circle, grassed us up to my mam.'

'Nosy cow. What did your mam say?'

'Oh, you know, "*I hope you're not heading the same way, our Dennis.*" Then she's like, "*I didn't see you doing a lot of revision back in June.*" Never off my flipping case.'

Michael pulled a face. 'Tell me about it. Mind you,' he chuckled, 'we *didn't*, did we?'

'Didn't what?'

'Revise.'

'*I* did. We *all* did, up in your room, remember?'

'Ha! We were hammered, my man, big time.'

'Not always.'

'*Not always.* We done a couple hours' genuine revision, if that. In a month. Two hours in a month tops, plus we were often somewhat rat-arsed in the examination room. We're looking at straight zeds, my friend.'

'Faxake, don't say that. My mam . . .'

'*My mam.*' Michael snorted. 'Listen, Dennis, what's it *matter*, huh? How many GCSEs do you need to be a packer at Wicklow's? You're doing it *now*, for Pete's sake. All you need is more hours and your life can be like it's been all summer.'

'Yeah I *know*, but Mam's got her heart set on me going to *uni*, see? Packing at Wicklow's is going to be like an *anticlimax* to her, know what I'm saying?'

Michael knew exactly what his friend was saying, but before he could say so Tim came boogying out of Virgin. He danced across the pavement watching his feet and waving his arms, scattering pensioners like confetti. 'Sorry I'm late, guys: bit of a run-in with Mater.'

'You too?'

'Oh yeah. "*Out again is it, slouching round town spitting and swearing. Seems you don't give a damn about those results looming; I hope it's because you know you've done well, blah, blah, blah . . .*"'

They laughed and nodded, moving away from the post office, down towards Market Square where the Midborough Wine Circle sat twitching and squabbling as they waited to be of service.

Five

'Morning.' Dennis grinned at the quartet on the wall. 'Is it me, or am I looking at four seriously thirsty guys?' He plonked down beside Digby who growled, 'Sixteen. Think it's all in front of you, right?'

Dennis nodded. 'I have seen the future, Digby old lad, and it is a world a-glitter with promise.'

'That's what you foggin' think. Listen. I was a chef, right? A qualified chef. I've created banquets out of stuff you don't even know exists. Stuff that costs a fortune. Truffles. Caviar. Nightingales' bleedin' tongues . . .'

'Come *off* it, you plank. Nightingales' *tongues*? You must think I just got here.'

Digby looked as haughty as a man can with a week's growth of stubble and a stink like a blocked drain. 'I'm *telling* you, you peasant, it was nightingales' tongues at a hundred and twelve quid an ounce.'

'That's not nightingales' tongues,' sniped Tim from further along the wall, 'that's dope. And talking of dopes, why don't you boogy on over to Thresher for a refresher. I've got the dosh.'

Digby leaned forward so he could eyeball the boy.

'I'll boogy Thresherward in my own good time, young man, and in the meantime I'll finish instructing your deeply ignorant friend in the ways of the world.' He turned back to Dennis. 'Where was I?'

'Banquets.'

'Oh yes, so I'd prepare these banquets – quail eggs, asparagus tips, lobster thermidor and so forth . . . taking hours and hours over it, you know, making everything perfect, and d'you know what I was thinking the whole time?'

'Astound me.'

'I was thinking what they'd amount to tomorrow, all these sumptuous dishes with their sauces and glazes and garnishes and what–not.'

'Yeah? What's that, then?'

'Shite.'

'Uh: well yeah, OK, but that's not . . . I mean, there's the *enjoyment*, isn't there? First.'

Digby shook his head. 'You've not been *listening*, son. The point is that no matter how much trouble you've taken, it all turns to shite in the end, and it's the same with life. Sooner or later everything turns to shite.'

'D'you really believe that?'

'Certainly. If it isn't true, what's a brilliant chef doing sitting on a wall with rotting feet and seven pence in his pocket?'

'I'll tell you what he *isn't* doing.' This from Yomper. 'He isn't relieving young Tim of his surplus cash and taking his ragged old ass down the grog shop. And I'll tell you what'll happen if he isn't on his way five seconds from now. Five seconds, then I'm gonna rip his head off and deposit *my* last banquet down the inside of his fat neck.'

'All *right*, Yomper,' soothed Digby, rising to his feet. 'Message received and understood, which is more than can be said for mine to our young friend. I cast the pearls of my wisdom before him and I know by his *face* he hasn't a clue what I've been talking about.' He sighed and stuck out a grubby palm. 'Come on then, Tim: divvy up. Sun'd be well over the yard-arm if we ever *saw* any flippin' sun around here.'

Six

'Oh hi . . . is this Mrs Wethouse . . . Westhouse, I mean?'

'Yes, I'm Mrs Westhouse. Who's calling?'

'You won't remember me, Mrs Westhouse. I came to you once for part of the summer hols. With Roger. Is he there?'

'Roger's in Greece with his father. Which summer are we talking about, because I don't recall Roger's having anybody to stay while he's been at –'

'It's Mark, Mrs Westhouse. Mark Penfold.'

'Good lord! Of *course* I remember you, Mark, but it must be . . . you were both at *Malsis,* for goodness' sake. It must be five, six years ago.'

'That'd be about right, Mrs Westhouse. I've never forgotten though, it was the best three weeks of my life.'

'*Surely* not?'

'Yeah, I'm not kidding . . . in fact, that's really why I'm calling. I realize this is the most awful cheek, but I was wondering if I might come again.'

'Come *again*? What do you . . . I told you, Roger isn't here. Why would you want . . . ?'

'*Please*, Mrs Westhouse. I'm in trouble. I can't go home. I need somewhere to be for a while, just a few days, and I remembered you and Mr Westhouse, how nice you both were to me. I'd be no trouble, honestly.'

'Is it your father, Mark? I remember your seeming a little in awe of your father that summer.'

'Awe? I wouldn't put it quite like that, Mrs Westhouse, but yes, it's my father. *Everything*'s my blasted father, alwas wis, alwis . . . always will be. Sorry.'

'Mark, are you all right? You sound a bit slurry, you haven't *taken* anything, have you?'

'Taken? No no, not in the way you mean, Mrs . . . look, *can* I come, just for a while? I won't be any trouble, honestly.'

'You said. Where are you calling from?'

'Pitney Forum, rectum of the universe.'

'Never heard of it.'

'West Country. I'm at school here. The Abbeyfield. Listen, ignore the rectum bit, I ought not to have . . . not to a lady. Kind lady like you. Can I come?'

'It's a long way, Mark. Two hundred miles, I should think. How will you get here?'

'Train.'

'When, today?'

'You mean you're letting me come?'

'Yes, Mark, you can come, but are you sure you're fit to travel? You sound . . . tight.'

'Tight? Oh, *hammered*, you mean. No, no, I'm not hammered. Not tight. Tired, that's all. So I'll see you sometime tonight, Mrs Westhouse. And thanks. Thank you very, very much. I knew *you*'d understand. Knew *you* wouldn't let me down.'

'Yes, well I hope I shan't regret it, that's all. Do be careful, and I'll see you soon. Goodbye.'

'Bye. Mrs Wethouse. Westhouse. Bye.'

Seven

Nobody christens their kid Cow. Nobody. Irving's his real name. Cow's a nickname they gave him when he was a milkman. His surname is True, and so is this story.

It's five to five on a dark, cold January morning in 1992. The milk float has open sides and Cow sits freezing in coat, scarf and mittens, trying to concentrate on steering the float between icy patches on the road. There's no other traffic and the float'll only do twenty but it's still not easy. He can't feel his feet, the mittens make his hands clumsy, he's only had two hours' kip and the Red Stripe he was still glugging at one this morning has left him with a pounding headache.

Cow delivers milk but never drinks it. He's been a Red Stripe man from the age of ten, when he'd sit for hours with a can in a dim corner of Pluto's, his father's so-called club. At ten years old he should have been in bed, but the thumping reggae beat that shook the house seven nights a week made sleep impossible and you know what they say: if you can't beat 'em, join 'em. Irving's mother was long gone and his dad was too busy to notice, so every night little Irving joined 'em. It didn't help him shine at school, and he left on his sixteenth birthday with a cry of relief and no certificates.

He got jobs though. Lots of jobs. Shelver in a supermarket, cleaner at a fast-food joint, carwash operative, door-to-door salesman of household cleaning products, assistant cook in an old-folks' home, tent erector, driver's mate on a breadvan, breadvan driver. Most he lost through drinking, some he walked away from.

So now he's a milkman. He drives drunk a lot of the time, but the vehicle is slow and there's little traffic so he manages. He's been at it six years, by far the longest he's ever kept a job, and he's reasonably content on this freezing January morning in spite of his smarting eyes and aching brain. His luck will run out as he tries to negotiate this next bend and falls asleep halfway round but he doesn't know it yet. He's dreaming a line of Ram Goat Liver as the float hits the ice and starts to drift sideways.

The street he's on is the poshest on Cow's round. In fact, it isn't a street it's a grove, Rowan Grove, and the house he's zeroing in on, number seven, is a des res with flash French doors giving on to a large, immaculate lawn that runs right out to the pavement. In milder weather the float would probably bog down halfway across the lawn, but frost has made the ground iron-hard and the little wheels roll over the crisp short turf unobstructed as Cow dreams on. In no time at all the vehicle reaches the French doors, crashes through, and delivers two hundred and eighty pints directly on to the lounge carpet.

Cow's case comes up at the beginning of February. He gets a driving ban, a fine and the sack. He applies for jobs but his case has been on telly and in the papers so there's no chance. In March he's evicted from his flat because he can't pay the rent. Homeless, he drifts to Midborough. The Wine Circle doesn't see TV or the papers. Its members know nothing about Cow's little accident and they wouldn't care if they did. He shows up with a bottle and it isn't a milk bottle so he's a member. He's been with them nine years and it seems like yesterday. Amazing how time flies when you're having fun.

Eight

The taxi pulled over and stopped. 'Here y'are, son, the Westhouse place. That'll be two-sixty.'

'Are you sure? I could've sworn it was somewhere in the three hundreds.'

The driver shook his head. 'The *fare,* sonny, I'm talking about the fare. Two-sixty. The *house* is 331.'

'Oh yes, of course. Sorry.' The boy dug out a handful of coins, found three pounds. 'Keep the change.'

'Ta.'

He watched till a bend extinguished the tail-light, then turned. The hawthorn hedge was less high than he remembered, the five-bar gate less wide. The ceramic plaque on the top rail still read Meldilorn. *'It's the name of a planet, darling,'* his friend's mother had said in answer to his question. *'C.S. Lewis.'*

The lever was as stiff as ever, but at least he could reach it without standing on the bottom rail. He pushed open the gate and jerked his head aside as a halogen lamp flared. *That's new.* He was closing the gate behind him, scrunching on gravel when the lamp died and a voice called, 'Sorry about that, Mark. You *are* Mark, I hope.'

He pushed the catch home and turned. The halogen had left a floating green blob and he could scarcely see her. 'Yes it's all right, Mrs Westhouse, it's only me.' He walked towards her, blinking the blob away. 'I'm sorry to show up at this time of night. Bloody train stopped for twenty-five minutes in the middle of nowhere. Vandalism to overhead cables or something.'

'It doesn't matter, Mark. You didn't leave your bag in the taxi, did you?'

'Bag?' He wiped his feet on the mat, stepped on to chequered tiles. 'There isn't a bag I'm afraid, Mrs Westhouse. Couldn't access my stuff, you see. Not easily.'

'Never mind, come on through. There's hot chocolate and I'll put something on a tray. You must be hungry.'

'No.' He followed her, shaking his head. 'I'm not a bit hungry, honestly. Chocolate sounds good though.'

The room looked familiar but seemed to have shrunk like everything else, including his hostess. She turned, smiling. 'Are you sure? I never met a growing boy who wasn't permanently ravenous, and you've certainly done some growing.'

He smiled. 'Funny, I was just thinking how much *smaller* everything seems.'

16

'Including me, I expect.'

'Uh . . . well, since you mention it.' He grinned ruefully. 'But I really *don't* want food, thanks.'

'Fine. Find a comfy chair and I'll get the chocolate.'

They faced each other in armchairs, a coffee table between them. There's something comforting about hot chocolate even on a warm night, and Mark relaxed a little as he sipped his. Mrs Westhouse gave him a few minutes then smiled brightly. 'You said something on the phone about trouble, Mark. D'you want to talk about it?'

Mark pulled a face. 'It's a bit complicated, Mrs Westhouse. I don't want to seem rude, but can we leave it till tomorrow? It's just that it's been a long day and my brain's packed up.'

'Of course, I'm sorry.' She leaned forward, topped up his cup from the silver pot, smiled at him through the steam. 'Look, if you're going to be here for a few days I think you'd better call me Marigold. Mrs Westhouse is a bit of a mouthful and you're not a little boy any more.'

'OK.' He smiled. 'I didn't know that was your name. Marigold. It's pretty.'

'It's ghastly. Roger's always been embarrassed by it, which I suppose is why he didn't tell you.'

'No, I like it. Really. Does Mr Westhouse call you Marigold?' *Can't remember him calling her that.*

She laughed. 'Mr Westhouse doesn't call me *anything* nowadays, Mark, we're divorced.'

'Oh, I'm sorry . . . I'd no idea. Didn't you say Roger was in Greece with him?'

'That's right. Roger goes away with his father every

17

summer.' She smiled. 'You needn't look so glum, dear, Robert and I don't *hate* each other or anything. It's all very civilized.'

Mark shook his head. 'I didn't mean to pry, Mrs . . . Marigold.' He shrugged. 'It's just that I liked him when I was here before. Wished he was *my* father, in fact.'

'Yes, well.' She sighed. 'Some men are model fathers and lousy husbands, Mark, and that's something *I*'d rather not talk about.'

'Sorry.'

'No.' She shook her head. 'I wasn't getting at you. Come on, I'll show you your room and dig out a set of Roger's pyjamas, then you can shower and get some sleep.'

He remembered the room. Remembered it bigger. Knew the curtained window looked out over an orchard and some tumbledown glasshouses. There was a little cut-glass jar on the bedside table with sprigs of peppermint and rosemary in it. She'd have placed it there earlier, when she knew he was coming. Gone down the garden, picked the herbs, put them in water. It was typical of her, of her thoughtfulness. He got into bed and lay on his side, gazing at the jar, noticing how its prisms caught the lamplight, making rainbows. After a minute he turned out the lamp, rolled on to his back and closed his eyes. *Marigold*, he murmured. *Marigold*.

Nine

The floor was ram-jam packed. The girl Dennis thought he was dancing with seemed to have attached herself to some guy of about eighteen with a face like a corpse, or maybe the strobes were making him look that way. Either way he was too big for Dennis, and in any case Dennis was dying from a combination of heat, beat and vodka on top of the day's lager. He waded through the crowd and headed for the toilets, hoping some sips of cold water would stop him throwing up.

The way to the basins was blocked by mirror-hoggers fixing their hair. Dennis crept along the row, looking for a gap. A volcano was bubbling up in his stomach. He tried to think about something else but there was no chance. His yelp of warning moved a guy with over-gelled hair and he dived in, grabbed the basin's rim with both hands and sprayed the mirror with used vodka under pressure. Gell-bonce backed off with a cry of disgust, flicking flecks of puke off his leather jacket with his nails. 'Mucky young bleeder!' he cried. 'What the eff you *doing* in here anyway, you're under-age.'

Feeling much better, Dennis was rinsing his mouth with cold water. 'Young for my age is all,' he gargled, 'wanna see my birth cert?' A mate of Michael's dad had done some birth certificates on his scanner. They were good as well.

Gell–bonce shook his head. 'Seen your flaming *dinner*, kid, don't wanna see nothing else of yours.' He was scrubbing the front of his jacket with a fistful of paper towels. 'I oughta kick your ass round the block.'

'Aye,' grunted a guy at the next mirror. 'And I ought to help you and all.' He'd got a bit splashed and wasn't amused. Dennis was still pretty wrecked, but not to where he couldn't see bother building up. 'Sorry, guys.' He clasped his belly and looked rueful. 'Got a pill from a guy, don't know what.'

Gell–bonce snorted. 'Bloody barmy then, could be dead.'

'Might happen yet,' growled the second guy, who'd taken his jacket off and was examining it under a strip-light.

Things could have gone from bad to worse if Tim and Michael hadn't picked that minute to show up. 'Dennis, you mammal, we thought you'd gone. What's up?'

Dennis shook his head. 'Not a thing. Just having a chat with these guys, thinking of splashing some water over the mirror here.'

'Eugh!' Michael screwed up his face. 'Which dirty –?'

'Me. Caught Hubert and Gilbert with a bit as well but they've been really nice, considering.'

'Hubert and Gilbert?' Michael looked at the youths, who were preparing to depart. These kids might only be sixteen but there were three of them now, and anyway fighting's a chucking-out offence. 'Are those real names or disc-jockey names or what?'

Gel-bonce shook his head. 'Never mind. You should

keep an eye on your mate. Popping dodgy gear, barfing over guys' clobber. Can be fatal.' He turned, headed for the door. The other lad nodded and followed, putting on his jacket.

When they'd gone Dennis said, 'Good timing, guys. They were psyching themselves up to give me a kicking.'

'Who *are* they?' demanded Tim, dashing a palmful of water on to the puke-streaked mirror. 'How d'you know their names?'

'I *don't*, you plank. Who'd christen a baby *Hubert* or *Gilbert*?'

'You made 'em up?'

'Course.'

'Like you weren't in enough bother already.'

'No chance of bother once you two showed, they'd be worried we'd spoil their jackets.'

Tim shook his head. 'Barmy.' The mirror was looking a lot better. 'Anyway,' punching the dryer button, turning his hands in the warm air, 'it's quarter to two, we better split. I don't know about you turkeys but I tend to get strife if I'm late in. Mam reckons she never sleeps till she hears the door.'

Michael shook his head. 'Mine's probably out herself.'

'Mine'll be out too,' growled Dennis, 'out like a light. Work and sleep, that's her life.' He felt a pang, wished the subject of mothers hadn't come up. You forget that crap for a while but it's there, under the sub-bass. *Is there such a thing as a permanent high?* If there was, Dennis meant to find it.

Ten

'Good morning, Mark. Sleep well?' She plugged in the grinder, switched on. A five-second burst was sufficient to pulverize the coffee beans and his brain. He winced, then smiled and nodded. 'Like a top thanks, Mrs Westhouse.'

'Marigold, remember?'

'Oh right. Marigold. It's wonderfully quiet here at night, isn't it, and dark. It's something I remember from before.'

'Yes, we're very lucky. What do you eat in the mornings, do you like a cooked breakfast?'

'I don't mind ... er ... Marigold. I'll have what you're having.'

'You won't get fat on that I'm afraid, I stick to black coffee.'

'Oh, then I'd like a helping of cornflakes if you have them.'

'Of course. Help yourself to coffee. There's cream in the small jug, milk in the other.'

When he'd shaken cornflakes into a bowl and poured milk over them, Marigold said, 'When did term end at The Abbeyfield, Mark?'

'Last Friday, but of course fellows doing GCSE can go as soon as they've sat their last exam. Some went off nearly a fortnight ago.'

'Yes, Roger was lucky that way. What about you – stuck to the bitter end, I suppose?'

'Well . . .' Mark stared at his upside-down reflection in the spoon. 'Actually, Marigold, that's the trouble I mentioned over the phone. I *would've* been stuck to the bitter end if I'd sat the rotten exams, but the fact is I didn't.'

'You mean you decided to skip the last one . . . it wasn't essential or something?'

'No.' He shook his head. 'I mean I was supposed to sit eleven subjects and I didn't take *any* of them.'

'But . . .' Marigold put down her cup. '*Why*, Mark? Were you ill, excused for some reason? I don't understand.'

Mark shook his head. 'I don't either, Marigold. Not really. I wish I could say I *was* excused for some legitimate reason but I wasn't. I was all set to take them, I'd revised and everything. Then when the time came I couldn't. Just *couldn't*. It might have been a sort of rebellion thing I suppose, against my father. It felt a bit like that, I mean he was in my mind when I took the decision. That purple, permanently apoplectic face that has terrified me all my life. His rage . . . no, that's not quite right . . . his *derision* when I told him at Easter I wanted to act. *Be* an actor, I mean. The sheer *ignorance* of his reaction. *"All actors are queer,"* that's what he said. *"A crowd of prancing nancy-boys contributing nothing useful to society and being grossly overpaid for it."* No son of his, and so forth.' He put down the spoon and looked at Marigold. 'The thing is, he's been on my back for about two years over those GCSEs. *"Three things count in life,*

Mark: qualifications, qualifications and qualifications. I had none, and you'll never know what it's cost me to get where I am today. And you needn't think just because you're the boss's son there's a cushy little number reserved for you within the Organization whether you turn out to be an academic success or not, because there isn't. Nobody gave me a leg up, and I'm damned if I'll give you one."' Mark pulled a face. 'That's how he speaks to me, Marigold, how he's *always* spoken. Do you wonder I thought I'd died and gone to heaven the summer I stayed here?'

His hostess didn't reply immediately. She refilled her cup and sipped coffee, frown-lines creasing the skin between her eyebrows. Presently she asked, 'Do your parents know where you are, Mark?'

'No. They'll know I'm not at school because I bunked off when the exams started and the Head will have called them, but it won't occur to them that I might be here.'

'So you're telling me you walked out of school . . . what, a month ago? Your people must be *frantic*, Mark. I insist you call them at once, tell them you're safe and well.'

Mark smiled bitterly. 'I doubt whether Father cares whether I'm safe or not, Marigold. I'd be distinctly *un*safe if I were anywhere within his reach.'

Marigold looked at him. 'Even if that's true, Mark, there's your mother. She cares far more about you than about some silly exams. Call her.'

The boy shook his head. 'She'd punch in 1471, get this number.'

'There's a way to prevent that and you know it. *The*

caller withheld his number. You mustn't be deceitful with me, Mark.'

'Sorry, Marigold, I don't mean to be deceitful but I'm scared. Scared of what I've done. If I call Mum, can I stay a few more days, just till I decide what to do?'

'If you call straight away, yes.' She frowned. 'As a matter of interest, where have you been staying since you walked out of school?'

'Oh, there's a small hotel, a pub really, in Pitney Forum. I took a room there.'

'Wasn't that a bit expensive, Mark? For a month?'

Mark looked rueful. 'Cost me practically everything I had; irony is, my father probably *owns* the damned pub.'

'Hmmm.' She looked at him. 'I'm going to church, and I'd be happier if you were to make that call before I leave. Is that all right?'

'Sure, Marigold, no problem. In fact I'll do it this minute.' He smiled. 'Stay and listen if you like.'

'I'll do nothing of the sort, young man. I'll be upstairs. You be sure and set your poor mother's mind at rest and I'll pop back before I leave.'

'OK.'

When he heard her footsteps on the stairs he tiptoed swiftly through into the room they'd occupied last night. He'd noticed some decanters and glasses on a small alcove table there. He'd thought it prudent to make do with chocolate at the time but it hadn't been easy, and if he absolutely *had* to go through with this call, he absolutely *must* put a shot of something warming inside him first.

Eleven

Sunday morning, half-eight. The Clissolds round a table splashed with sunlight from the kitchen window. Susan squinted across at her elder son. 'What time did you get in last night, our Dennis?'

Dennis stirred his tea. 'Oh I dunno – around twelve, I think.' His head ached and the sun wasn't helping.

'Oooh, you big liar!' This from twelve-year-old Jimmy, spreading jam on a slice of toast. 'It was quarter-past two.'

'Was it heck, you creepazoid. How would *you* know?'

'I know 'cause you woke me up coming in the room and I looked at the clock. Oh-two-fifteen, it said.'

'Get *lost*, stirring it up as usual.'

'It was certainly later than twelve, Dennis,' put in his mother. 'I didn't go up till about ten to, and I don't sleep straight away, and *I* never heard you come in.'

Dennis's throat felt parched. He gulped some tea, put down his mug. 'OK, so it was late. What's the big deal?'

'Big deal,' said Marie. 'What's the big deal, what's the big *wheel*, what's the big *seal*.' At nine, she was a collector of interesting expressions. Her mother silenced her with a look and eyeballed Dennis.

'The *big deal*, as you call it, is that you're only sixteen. When *I* was sixteen I'd never seen the inside of a club.'

'They didn't *have* clubs then, Mam. Only the sort you bash guys over the head with. It was the *Stone* Age for Pete's sake.'

'It was the *seventies*, you cheeky young beggar. Midborough was full of clubs, including the one you're so keen on, only it wasn't called Hackers then, it was The Little Fat Black Pussy-Cat. I'd have loved to go to The Little Fat Black Pussy-Cat, but I'd to be in by eleven. A minute after and your grandad'd be standing on the step, looking at his watch.'

'Yeah, well.' Dennis drained his mug, refilled it from the pot. 'That was then. Times change, Mam. All the guys stay out late, doesn't do 'em any harm.'

'Oh, I don't know about that.' Susan shook her head. 'There wasn't the violence back then, our Dennis, or the truancy. I think it does a *lot* of harm when you're sixteen, gallivanting to the early hours, not to mention this ecstasy business.'

Dennis shook his head. 'I'm not into that, Mam. Never touch pills.'

'No, and I hope you never will. Anyway.' She retied the cord of her quilted dressing-gown, stood up, started clearing the table. 'Things might be changing down Hackers soon, it's been bought out.'

'How d'you mean, bought out?'

'It was in the paper, some big brewery's bought it.' She smiled. 'You never know, they might decide to call it The Little Fat Black Pussy-Cat again.'

Twelve

'Garton 3396, Jane Penfold speaking.'

'Hello, Mumsie.'

'*Mark?* Is this Mark?'

'Yes, it's me. I'm sorry I haven't been –'

'Where *are* you, Mark? What's happened?'

'Nothing's *happened,* Mother, I'm perfectly all right.'

'But where *are* you, darling, where have you *been*? What happened at *school*?'

'I'm sorry, Mother, I'm not going to tell you where I am; only that I'm safe and well. Nothing happened at school, except that I found I couldn't face the exams. I've been staying at the Fleece in the village. I'm somewhere else now.'

'*Why*, Mark? Why won't you tell me where you are? Don't you realize how frantic we've been? Your father went so far as to accost the Chief Constable at a private dinner to ask him to order an investigation.'

'Yes, I can easily imagine Father doing something like that.'

'He *loves* you, Mark.'

'Then all I can say is he's had a damned odd way of showing it. At any rate I don't love *him*, in fact he's the reason I flunked out of school.'

'Come *home*, darling. It doesn't matter about school, honestly. We just want you here, safe and sound.'

'*You* want that, Mother, *he* doesn't. I know him. He hasn't been *concerned*, he's been *furious*. He wants me within ranting range, and I'm not going to oblige him.'

'I'll *talk* to him, darling. He'll listen to me.'

'He listens to *nobody*, Mumsie, you know that. All my life you've tried to protect me from him: it's impossible. I'm truly sorry to be doing this to you, but I won't come home till I'm as big as he is. I've got to go now.'

'*No,* darling, don't hang up, *please.* You don't know what a mother goes through in the middle of the night, imagining –'

'I'll phone when I can, Mumsie, so you'll know I'm all right. Hug Jess for me. Bye.'

'*Mark . . . ?*'

Thirteen

'Who's Jess, Mark?' Marigold Westhouse came smiling through the doorway as Mark hung up.

He looked at her. 'You said you weren't going to listen.'

'I *haven*'t listened, silly. I heard you say hug Jess as I came downstairs, that's all.'

'Right. Jess is my sister, Jessicca.'

'Oh yes, now I remember. She's older, isn't she?'

'Ah-ha. Nineteen. She's at Oxford.'

'Doing well?'

'Better than her brother.'

29

'I didn't mean that.'

'No, but it's true. She was brighter than me from the start. My father's always been annoyed about that. He's one of those men who think brains are wasted in a woman.'

'Yes, I know the type. I assume you were speaking to your mother. How was it?'

Mark shrugged. 'All right, I suppose. She's been worried, pretended Father has too but I know better. She asked where I was, of course.'

'And you didn't tell her.'

'No, Marigold, I didn't. I said I was safe and well, and that I'd phone from time to time.'

'Good. You don't fancy coming to church, do you?'

He shook his head. 'Not really, if that's all right.'

'Of course it is.' She smiled. 'Perhaps it's just as well. My showing up with a handsome young man might be enough to set tongues wagging. You know what villages are like.'

'Is that what I *am*, Marigold? A handsome young man?'

'Certainly you are, Mark. Let nobody tell you otherwise.' She looked at her watch. 'I must fly. You'll be all right, I suppose?'

'I'll be absolutely fine. Thought I'd mooch about the garden, see how much I've misremembered.'

'Good idea. I'll be back around twelve, I expect. Bye.'

'Bye, Marigold.'

Amazing how relaxed I feel with a drop of the lotion inside me. Marigold, just like that. I'll be calling Father Ralphie baby next.

30

Fourteen

'Dennis?'

'Mam.'

'I want you to do me a favour this morning, love. I'm not feeling too good and I thought I'd go back to bed for a bit. Will you take the kids down the park, keep 'em amused till dinnertime?'

'Aw, *Ma*-am.' Dennis lowered the sport section and scowled at her. 'I'm not exactly one hundred per cent myself, you know. I was going to chill out, read the papers, have a couple of coffees.'

'Mam says you've to take us down the park,' chirped Marie, 'so come on.' She was already pulling on her trainers.

Dennis sighed, folded the paper, hauled himself out of the armchair. 'OK, OK, no peace for the wicked. Get your shoes, our Jimmy, but I'm *not* hanging around that flipping playground all morning watching you two slide and swing. We'll go down the lake, have a boat.'

'*I'm* off on the swings,' asserted Marie. 'I'm having ten goes.'

'And I'll be boss of the roundabout,' said Jimmy, 'make it whizz. Boats're boring.'

'You'll both do what your big brother *tells* you to do,' snapped their mother. 'Do you hear, our Jimmy?'

'Yes, Mam.'

'Marie?'

'Yes.'

'Good.' She smiled wanly at Dennis. 'Thanks, love, you're saving my life. Have a nice time, all of you. Don't talk to strangers and I'll see you at dinnertime.'

It was a warm, sunny morning and there were a lot of people in the park. 'We'd better rush if you want to get on something,' said Dennis, 'playground'll be packed out.'

Jimmy looked at him. 'You said we couldn't *go* in the playground.'

'Yeah well, I've got something to do, our Jimmy. Something important. I won't be long, but I'm leaving you in the playground and I want you to keep an eye on Marie. All right?'

'Yeah, triffic.'

'I can keep an eye on *myself*,' muttered Marie. 'I don't need him spying on me every minute.'

Dennis shot her a warning look. 'You behave, or I'll take you with me and you won't get a go on *anything*. OK?'

'Big deal,' she growled.

There were kids in the playground, grans and big sisters on the benches, but the place wasn't full. Marie broke away, bagged the one free swing. Dennis held his brother back. 'Listen, don't get obsessed with that flaming roundabout and forget to look out for our Marie. I'll be about quarter of an hour and, if you're lucky, I might bring you something from Patel's.'

He watched the two children for a minute, then took the path across the playing field and left the park through its far gateway. Breakfast coffee hadn't shifted his headache and his throat still felt parched, but there was medicine down Patel's offie that was guaranteed to do the trick every time.

There were two customers. Dennis browsed the shelves till they'd gone, then carried two special lagers to the counter. The proprietor, a sad-looking man of about fifty with a drooping moustache, looked at him. 'How old are you, please?'

'You asked me that last time. The answer's still eighteen.'

'Yes, but you are no more than fifteen, sixteen. You will get me in trouble some of these days.'

'Listen.' Dennis leaned across the counter, spoke softly. 'I'm the customer, you're the shopkeeper. How're *you* supposed to know how old I am? You serve me, I pay and leave, end of story. On the other hand you could refuse to sell me what I want and I could come back with a few friends, and some of your stock might fall down, smash on the floor.'

'I have a dog.'

'Does he put fires out?'

He re-entered the park with the cans sticking out of his jacket pockets and sweetie bags bulging his jeans. Instead of going straight to the playground he left the path and waded through some overgrown rhododendrons to a dilapidated gazebo whose floor was covered by a slimy carpet of last autumn's fallen leaves. He plonked down on a bench, pulled out a can, opened it and drank, tilting his head right back.

'Aaaah!' He put the half-empty can on the bench and sat with his eyes closed, waiting for the medicine to work. The parched feeling had gone already: soon the headache would follow. In the rhododendrons a thrush was singing.

Nice. Bushes, breeze, birdsong. The three Bs. Brasso'd add a fourth, wouldn't he? Booze. Dennis smiled, remembering something Brasso had said once in an indignant voice when Digby called him an alkie. 'I only drink when I'm by myself or with somebody.' *Good, that.*

Fifteen

The garden was much as Mark remembered it, except that now the grass was far too long in the orchard. *Comes of having no man about the place.* He might ask Marigold about a mower, tackle the job himself.

The greenhouses were practically falling down and that was no big surprise: they'd been dilapidated when he was eleven. He sauntered over broken glass, picking things up and putting them down. *Shame. Could have been fixed up at one time. Too late now.*

Back in the orchard he picked a greengage and sat down with his back against a tree. The fruit was tart, not fully ripe. He swallowed the first bite and threw the rest into the long grass. It was quite hot in the sun. He closed his eyes.

Marigold. Not bad-looking for a chap's mother, and she

thinks I'm handsome. A handsome young man. What if . . .
He smiled dreamily. *What if I just stayed? It's a fine place.*
Meldilorn. He chuckled. *Master of Meldilorn, why not?*
Roger might take a dim view, I suppose, stepfather his own
age. But it happens. It happens.

Mark dozed in the sunshine till thoughts of his father
warned him it was time for a fresh application of the
lotion. He rose, looked at his watch and strolled back to
the house.

It was a good whisky, a single malt. Trouble was, by
the time he'd taken a couple of slugs the level in the
decanter was worryingly low. *Does she touch it herself, I*
wonder. Will she notice?

Deciding it wasn't worth the risk he carried the
decanter through to the kitchen and topped it up with
tap water. It seemed not to alter the colour much and,
anyway, whiskies come in a variety of shades so he
helped himself to a further nip, and then another to
compensate for the dilution factor. It still tasted fine
though. He put it back on the little table, stretched
himself out on the sofa, scrolled through his mind and,
finding no trace of his father, fell asleep.

Sixteen

The playground was a heck of a lot busier than when
he'd left it an hour ago, but there was no sign of either
Jimmy or Marie. Dennis had investigated every ride,

35

wading through shrill, milling kids. Now he stood at the edge trying to think – an activity that threatened to restart his headache.

Fifth B. No – fifth and sixth: Bastard Brats. If that Jimmy's taken our Marie on the lake by himself I'll kill him, I will.

He was about to head for the lake when a hand plucked at his sleeve. 'Excuse me?' He turned to find himself looking at somebody's gran. 'Yeah?'

'You seem to be looking for somebody. Is your name Dennis?'

'Yes it is, how d'you know?'

'There was an accident, about half an hour ago, on the slide. A little girl.'

'*Accident?*' Fear blew the fog off his mind. 'Was she called Marie? What *happened*?'

The old lady shook her head. 'I don't know her name, sorry. She'd been playing at running *up* the slide, there was a tussle with somebody at the top and she fell. I didn't really see, I was watching my grandson. There was a scream, and I saw her lying under the slide. Somebody with a mobile called the ambulance. There was a boy, he was hysterical. Kept shouting for you. *"Dennis, Dennis where are you?"* When the ambulance came they put both children in the back. The little girl was on a stretcher, I think she'd hurt her head.'

'Oh heck . . . flipping heck. Where'd it *take* 'em, the ambulance?'

The gran shrugged. 'I'm not sure, love, but I expect it'd be the Infirmary. That's the accident and emergency place, but listen . . .' He'd turned, ready to run all the way to the Infirmary where the three of them had been born. The old lady looked at him. 'Try not to worry, love, she's probably all right. Children are resilient, you know: they bounce.'

'Yeah, right. Thanks.'

It took him fourteen minutes at a dead run to reach the Infirmary. He had to stop just inside the gateway and throw up the lager. His eyes were watering so much he could hardly find Reception. There was puke down his front and the volunteer looked a bit disapproving, directing him to Ward Nine. It was up two flights of stairs. He found it, walked in and groaned. His mother had got there before him.

Seventeen

The phone woke Mark. He turned over, shielded his eyes from the bright window, peered at his watch. Five past twelve. *Ought to thank the bloody thing I suppose, wouldn't do for Marigold to walk in and find me zonked out on the settee. Might think I'd been at her booze.*

It was still ringing. Some people are *so* persistent. He sat up, stretched and yawned. *No point my picking up though, is there? Wonder where she is, she said twelve.* He got up, wandered out to the hallway. Whoever it was was still trying. *OK.* He smiled. *Your choice.* He picked up.

'Lashford 646487, Mark speaking.'

'Who?' Man's voice, sharp. Mark took an instant dislike.

'Mark.'

'Is Mrs Westhouse there?'

'No.'

'This *is* Lashford 646487?'

'Yes.'

'Then who am I speaking to?'

'I *told* you, *Mark*.'

'Friend of Roger's, are you?'

'Roger's in Greece.'

'Yes, I *know*.'

'I'm a friend of Marigold's. A good friend. A *very* good friend, in fact. Who shall I say called?'

'It doesn't matter, I'll try again later.'

'If it's about double-glazing, I shouldn't bother.'

'Double-*glazing*?' The guy spluttered some words Mark didn't catch and slammed down the phone. Less than a minute later Marigold walked in.

'Sorry to be late, Mark.' She put her bag on a side-table, stepped out of smart shoes into scuffed flatties. 'Churchdoor chatter. Did you manage to entertain yourself all right?'

'Yes thanks.' He grinned. 'Never a dull moment, in fact. Good service?'

'Some dull moments there, I'm afraid. Still,' she smiled, 'one shows one's face, it's expected.'

'Right.' He nodded. 'Have you got a mower, Marigold? Didn't see one when I was pottering.'

'Yes, it's in the garage. Petrol-driven monster. Why?'

'Grass is a bit long in the orchard, I could have a go at it if you like.'

'That would be kind, Mark.' She smiled. 'Tell you what: why don't you get acquainted with the mower while I do us a spot of lunch? I thought a salmon salad with boiled new potatoes.'

'Sounds wonderful.'

'Fine. I'll call you when it's ready.'

The machine was similar to one Mark's father's gardener used. There was even petrol in it. He trundled it across to the orchard, started it up and steered it between the laden fruit trees, cutting swathes through the tangle. He'd done nearly half by the time lunch was ready. The motor drowned Marigold's voice so that she had to come right down the garden to attract his attention.

He switched it off and followed her up to the house. She seemed displeased about something and he thought it must be that, but when he came down from washing his hands she said, 'Why didn't you tell me somebody phoned while I was out, Mark?'

He shrugged. 'I forgot, sorry. Was it important?'

Marigold shook her head. 'It wasn't particularly *important*, Mark, but that's not the point. Charles says you were rude to him.'

'Charles?'

'Charles Seward, a friend. Says you were monosyllabic and pretended to believe he was selling double-glazing.'

'I *did* believe that, Marigold, because he refused to give his name. It's a trick salesmen use to catch punters on the hop, so to speak. As for being monosyllabic, I probably *was*. I'd dozed off in the orchard and was only half awake. I'm sorry if I came across as rude, I didn't mean to.'

'No, well.' She placed olive wood servers in the salad bowl. 'It might be as well in future to let it ring if I'm not here, or let Susan get it. Susan comes weekday mornings,' she added before he could ask, 'cleans up.'

'Oh.' He felt humiliated, like a kid who's been told off unjustly but daren't defend himself. He wanted to say, *'What about the orchard, all my hard work,'* but it sounded childish and irrelevant even to him. 'OK, Marigold, if you think that's best.' *She's right, too. I was rude, deliberately rude, and I don't know why really. Yes I do, it was the whisky. No more whisky then. She might have made me leave.*

'It isn't *quite* the end of the world, Mark.' He met her eyes and they were smiling. 'The orchard's looking heaps better already, so take that hangdog look off your face and heap your plate. You're going to need all your strength this afternoon, toiling under that sun.'

Eighteen

'How is she?' It didn't look good, little grey face on big white pillow, bandage like a Sikh turban. Marie's eyes were closed.

'Where the heck were *you*, Dennis? You were supposed to be looking after them.'

'I know, Mam. I popped over to Patel's for sweets. Wasn't gone ten minutes.'

'Ten *minutes*?' This from Jimmy in a chair on the far side of the bed. 'You big liar. It was half an hour at least. You must have went somewhere else.'

'No I didn't. And it's *gone*, not went.'

'Never mind our Jimmy's grammar, you daft beggar. Look at your sister: seven stitches, bruising, suspected concussion. *You* did that to her, our Dennis. Are you satisfied now?'

'*Satisfied* . . . what d'you mean, satisfied? You think I *wanted* this to happen? You think I *paid* someone to shove her off the slide? I'm as upset about this as you, Mam, but it isn't my fault. All I did was –'

'*Pop over to Patel's*,' finished his mother. 'I know you popped over to Patel's. What I *don't* know is why, though I can guess.'

'I *told* you, I went for sweets for them. Look.' He emptied his jeans pockets, dropped two bags on the bed. 'Liquorice allsorts, jelly babies.'

'Oooh, can I have –?' Jimmy reached across.

'No you *can't*, not here.' His mother snatched up the sweets, stowed them in her handbag, turned to Dennis. 'You got these for the kids: what for yourself?'

'Nothing, Mam.'

'Don't lie to me. You stink like a barman's rag, and look at the state of that T-shirt. D'you think I don't know that smell, or recognize drunk's upchuck when I see it? I'd seventeen years of it, Dennis. Seventeen years, trying to keep it from you what your father was; from our friends, from neighbours. And you stand there like a

41

clone of him, lying straight-faced while your sister lies unconscious because you couldn't wait to get to Patel's. *Lager*, that's what you got for yourself.' Her voice wavered, there were tears on her cheeks. 'I don't *know*, our Dennis. I don't know what to think, what to do. I don't *want* another Jim Clissold in my house. Won't *have* one, so if that's the direction you're heading in you'd better start looking for a place of your own.'

'*Mam*.' He reached for her but she stepped back.

'No, Dennis, I don't *want* to nestle against a pukey shirt, breathing your sour breath while you tell me how sorry you are, how you don't know what came over you, how things'll be different from now on.' She fished a tissue from her bag and dabbed at her face. 'You see I've *done* all that, over and over. Listened to it, let myself believe it, got another kick in the face for my trouble.'

'Mam, it's not like that, honestly. I'm not Dad, I'm not *hooked*: I like the odd can to chill out with, that's all. With my mates. Look: I'll pack it in, OK? I'll –'

'Ma-am?' Three pairs of eyes swung to the pillow where a fourth pair had flickered open. 'What's happening? I feel sick . . .'

Nineteen

Sunday is Digby's day for shopping. Cow christened him Digby because he reckons he looks like Dan Dare's sidekick in the old Eagle *comics. He's Darryl Farnsworth really.*

As a qualified chef, Digby always shops at Sainsbury's. He never has any money, but at Midborough Sainsbury's you don't need any. This is because the store was completely refurbished last year with many improvements. Digby's favourite improvement is the cafeteria, where tired shoppers can relax after their exertions with a pot of coffee and a simple meal.

It's got some thoughtful touches, this cafeteria. For instance there's a rack with copies of the day's newspapers so customers can have a read while their coffee cools. There are highchairs for babies and a play area for kids. There's even a trolley park where shoppers can leave their laden trolleys while they enjoy a nice rest. The trolley park is the focal point of Digby's expeditions.

What happens is this. Sunday mornings Digby, Yomper, Cow and Brasso gather behind the berberis and swap their clothes around so Digby ends up wearing all the cleanest stuff. You can't go in Sainsbury's looking like a tramp. The store opens at ten, but Digby waits till about half-eleven before making his way there, dangling a carrier bag.

The place is seething. The legions of the bored have turned up in force to while away the Sabbath in a trance of gawping and spending. Digby saunters across the busy car park to where empty trolleys stand in rows, handily adjacent to the plate-glass window of the cafeteria. He takes his time selecting a trolley, eyeing up the eaters and drinkers inside. The place is doing a steady trade and there are loaded trolleys in the trolley park. Digby wheels his empty trolley through the automatic doors, abandons it in the newspaper and magazine concession where the presence of many browsers renders him inconspicuous, strolls past the dry-cleaning bay and the heel bar, down towards the cafeteria and toilets.

The trick is to look dead casual while actually being acutely aware of everything that's going on. Where's the security man? There's always one somewhere. Is the woman behind the Customer Services counter busy? Is anybody looking at me, showing undue interest?

If something doesn't feel right, Digby will walk past the cafeteria without even glancing at it, wait in the toilets, try later. If it seems OK he'll saunter in and pretend to look for a table. Chances are, this time on a Sunday they'll all be taken. In any case he won't be the only one looking, so he won't stick out and that's crucial. The good thing is, everybody's looking out for number one. Nobody's bothered whether he gets a table or not.

The rest's easy if you don't panic. Quick check on the seated customers. Is somebody paranoid about her trolley, keeping an eye? If yes, go towards the counter as if one of the women there's your missus, try in a minute. If no, walk to the trolley park, roll one out and wheel it away. Don't act furtive, don't rush, but be ready to run if somebody shouts.

On this July Sunday morning nobody shouts. They're buttering toast, checking out the test score, keeping an eye on the kids. Digby wheels somebody's groceries through the automatic doors into the sunshine and away.

Sainsbury's, where good food costs less.

Twenty

Lady Penfold knocks timidly on the door of her husband's study. It is never a good idea to do this because

Sir Ralph is a busy man, even on a Sunday morning, but this bit of news won't wait.

'Yes, what is it?'

She opens the door a crack. 'That was Mark on the phone, dear. He's all right.'

'Is he, by golly?' Sir Ralph throws down the folder he'd been riffling through; its contents have put him in a good humour. 'Well come in, Jane, for goodness' sake: don't hover like a Jehovah's Witness. Where is the boy?'

'I don't know, dear.'

'What d'you mean, you don't know? Where was he phoning from?'

'He wouldn't say. He's safe and well, that's what he called to tell us.'

'Humph! Considerate of him. What about school, his exams?'

'He said . . . he couldn't face the exams, Ralph. He's been staying at the village inn.'

'Couldn't face . . . ?' Sir Ralph's neck reddens, his amiable mood evaporates. 'Suppose he'd had to face poverty, Jane, as I did? Claw and kick his way up out of the gutter? Could he have faced that, d'you think?'

Lady Jane sighs. 'I'm sure I don't know, dear.'

'You don't know. Well I do, and the answer's no. He'd have stayed in the gutter, his children would've been born there and none of them would ever have come within twenty miles of a place like The Abbeyfield. The trouble with your son, Jane, is that he doesn't know how lucky he is.'

'I'm sure *our* son knows that only too well, Ralph: goodness knows you told him often enough.'

45

'What the devil d'you mean? Are you saying –?'

'I'm saying Mark had your humble beginnings rammed down his throat before he was old enough to know what you were talking about. All his life you've assaulted him with the contrast between his start and yours and you refuse to see that Mark bears no responsibility for that contrast. You're infatuated with your own success, Ralph Penfold, like many self-made men, and it's made a bully of you. Now the poor boy daren't even tell us where . . . where . . .' She breaks down, buries her face in a handkerchief.

'Oh now look, Jane, don't . . .' He reaches for her but she shrugs him off with a small mew of protest. 'Don't upset yourself. He's safe and well, he told you so. He'll come home when he's hungry, like somebody's blasted pussy-cat, and in the meantime here's something to celebrate.' He picks up the folder, strokes it. 'I've finally got that damned club.' He smiles. 'Hackers, Jane: it's in the bag.'

Twenty-one

Lunch over, Mark and Marigold carried coffee through to the lounge and split the *Observer* between them. Mark browsed through the sport section while his hostess looked through business. He was halfway down the cricket scores when she said, 'There's a bit here about your father, Mark.'

'Oh?' *Obituary, I hope.* 'What about him, Marigold?'

'Says Penfold Breweries plc has acquired a controlling interest in something called Garage, which operates a chain of clubs in city centres. It *is* him, isn't it: Penfold Breweries?'

Mark nodded grimly. 'That's Father, all right. Champagne moment for him, Marigold, he's got Midborough sewn up at last.'

'What d'you mean, sewn up?'

Mark pulled a face. 'For years Penfold's controlled every pub, every licensed premise in the town except Hackers, which is Midborough's only dance club. It was independent at first and my father was bent on buying it up, not because it was making a lot of dosh but *because* it was independent. Its very existence outside his control irritated him. He took it for granted he'd get it in the end, and he was furious when the owner sold it to Garage. So what does he do, he buys Garage. That's my father, Marigold: has to be boss of everything.'

'Hmmm.' She smiled across at him. 'Might this be a good time for you to go home though, Mark: champagne flowing, father feeling expansive?'

Mark shook his head. 'There's *no* good time to go to Garton Hall, Marigold. Not for me.' He looked at her. 'Why: d'you want rid of me?'

'No, no.' She shook her head. 'I just thought, you know: you're going to have to go sooner or later so why not now, while your father's flushed with triumph and fine wine?'

'Triumph brings out the worst in him,' growled

Mark, 'and I was speaking figuratively when I mentioned a champagne moment. He's teetotal.'

'What?' Marigold looked incredulous. 'Sir Ralph Penfold, Chairman of Penfold Breweries plc, *teetotal*?'

Mark nodded. 'Closely guarded secret, Marigold. Fakes it with cold tea at functions.'

'Good grief.'

'Brought up Methodist, you see. Went into brewing to spite my grandfather but couldn't bring himself actually to drink.'

'How extraordinary.'

'Not really. We all rebel against our parents.'

'Yes, I suppose we do.' She smiled. 'Does that mean you're set to become an inveterate boozer, Mark?'

'Me?' He shook his head. 'No chance, Marigold. Can't stand the stuff.'

Twenty-two

They were keeping Marie in overnight, under observation. She cried when they had to leave. Susan stroked the little girl's hair and said, 'It's only one night, lovey, we're coming to take you home in the morning.' To Dennis she hissed, 'See what it does to your family? I hope you think it was worth it.'

I don't. Course I don't. He couldn't speak past the aching lump in his throat. They traipsed along a corridor and downstairs, Dennis behind so they wouldn't see his

48

brimming eyes as he tried to drive the image of that bandaged head from his mind. *I wish I'd never gone to rotten Patel's, my throat was dry that's all. I wish it was me in that bed. Wearing that bandage. I'm never gonna touch lager again. Ever.*

The infirmary car park was full so his mother had left the Micra on the road. Dennis usually rode in front with her but Jimmy got it today so he sat in the back, dabbing at his pukey T-shirt with a fistful of tissues, trying not to notice his mother watching him in the mirror. She and Jimmy exchanged occasional remarks but nobody spoke to him.

It was the same over lunch. Late lunch. Tuna, peas, tinned spuds; iced doughnuts for pudding. Jimmy asked if he could have Marie's doughnut and his mother said, 'She's not *dead*, our Jimmy, *no thanks to certain people*. She can have hers tomorrow, *if* she's not too poorly to eat.'

Dennis couldn't eat much. He'd changed out of his messed-up kit and splashed cold water on his face, but he still felt rough. When he pushed his plate away his mother murmured, '*Conscience*, Dennis?' He shook his head and mumbled something about his gut but she was probably right, partly anyway. He kept seeing Marie's face, grey against the white of the hospital pillow, but it wasn't just that. He was thinking about the GCSE results coming out as well. Michael's words echoed inside his skull. '*We're looking at straight zeds, my friend.*' Bit of an exaggeration maybe but not far out. Not far out. He pushed his chair back and got up.

'Where d'you think you're *going*?' asked his mother sharply. Dennis looked down at her and realized he didn't know: wasn't *going* anywhere really except away from her table, her accusing eyes. He didn't want to say this, or that he didn't know, so he gave the answer Dad used to give when he lived with them and she asked the same question.

'Out.'

Twenty-three

Monday morning, ten o'clock. Brilliant outside, sunlight through south-facing windows falling in bright rectangles on Marigold's lounge carpet.

Marigold was out, something about a pedicure. Mark had half-promised to weed and rake the driveway, but before that he must find out where she stashed the booze. Topping up with water's all right but you can only do it so many times. The stuff in the whisky decanter was looking decidedly anaemic in the morning light, and by lunchtime the cognac might be a bit wishy-washy too.

He'd plenty of time. After a nip or two of the cognac he started in the lounge and investigated a sideboard, a locked chest whose key was in the sideboard, and some drawers under a bookcase. No luck. It was inconceivable that the stuff in the decanters was all she had in the house, so he treated himself to another little snifter and moved to the breakfast room, singing to himself, and from there to the kitchen. There was no booze in either place, but a door in the kitchen gave on to a flight of stone stairs that descended into darkness.

Of course! He found the light switch and trotted down and there it all was, rows and rows of the filthy stuff, racked and neatly labelled. Most of it was wine, which was better than nothing, but right at the far end were enough bottles of a single malt to inundate half a county.

The acoustics weren't bad either: bit like the school showers in fact. He sang louder, switched from Blur to Pavarotti, threw out his chest and strutted. He was belting out 'Nessun Dorma' with an unopened bottle for a mike when he executed a half-turn and saw a woman halfway down the steps.

'Ah.' The echo of Pav's last note dwindled as Mark's memory lurched into motion. '*Susan comes weekday mornings, cleans up.*' He grinned and sketched a bow. 'Susan, that right?'

The woman neither stirred nor smiled. He'd half-decided she must be the Meldilorn Ghost when she did her Bart Simpson impression. 'Who the hell are *you*?'

He smiled. 'My name's Penfold, Susan. Mark Penfold. I'm staying with Mar . . . with Mrs Westhouse. I was sort of . . . *exploring*.'

'You were making an unholy din, yourself at home and off with a bottle of Mrs Westhouse's whisky as far as I can see. How do I know you're not a burglar? *Stay where you are!*' He'd taken a step towards her. She seized a bottle of gooseberries from a shelf beside her and made as if to shy it at him.

Mark stood still and raised his hands, palms towards

her. 'OK, it's OK, Susan.' He gazed up at her. 'How would I know your name if I were a burglar, and what sort of burglar sings opera at the top of his voice while robbing somebody's house?'

'Where's Mrs Westhouse then?'

He arched his brow. 'Don't you know?'

'I'm asking *you*.' She still hadn't smiled.

'Oh I *see*, you're testing me. All right. Mrs Westhouse is with her pedicurist. Her son, whose name is Roger, is in Greece with his father. Roger's father and Mrs Westhouse are divorced. Yesterday Mrs Westhouse went to church. While she was out, a friend, Charles Seward, phoned. I told him –'

'Yes, all right.' Susan returned the gooseberries to the shelf. 'Put the whisky back and come up. I'm sorry to be suspicious, but you can't be too careful these days and Mrs Westhouse ought to have told me she had a guest.' She peered down at him. 'Are you a nephew or something?'

Mark slid the bottle into its pigeon-hole and shook his head. 'I'm a friend of Roger's really. I stayed here once before, when I was a kid.' He climbed the stairs. Susan held the door, closed it when he was up. He smiled. 'Thanks, Susan, and I'm sorry if I gave you a fright. I'd better get out there: promised to tidy the driveway a bit. I'll see you later, I expect.'

Susan smiled faintly, perhaps to prove she could. 'I expect so, Mark.' He walked past her, holding his breath so she wouldn't smell the brandy.

Twenty-four

'Morning, Dennis,' greeted Michael, 'have I got news for you.'

'Never watch it. My mam does.'

'Not the *show*, you marsupial, I'm not talking about the show. I've got news.'

'Go on.'

'Hackers has changed hands.'

'That's history, Michael, not news. My mam told me yesterday. Some big brewery, she said.'

'*Some* big brewery? It's not *some* big brewery, you ruminant, it's *Penfold*. You know: guy has the big house out Garton way?'

'Yeah, Garton Hall. What of it?'

'Well, his outfit runs all the pubs round here and they say he's got a thing about under-age drinking.'

'So?'

'How d'you mean, *so*? How old are you, Dennis my man?'

'Same as you, you omnivore.'

'Exactly. We're both sixteen and we enjoy a few Vodka Red Bulls down Hackers, and now Hackers belongs to a guy who doesn't *believe* in selling booze to sixteen-year-olds. Know what I'm saying?'

Dennis shrugged. 'Yeah, I know what you're saying, but, like, it's *always* been illegal to sell us drink. Hell, it's illegal to even let us *in* Hackers, but we've managed.'

'Yeah, with bent birth certs, but what if this Penfold guy hires new Saint Peters: keen ones who really *look* at you and examine your cert? It could mean the end of our clubbing, my man.'

Dennis shook his head. 'Naah! We'll find a way, whatever happens. Don't worry about it.'

'I'll try not to. Let's go find the Circle.'

'Can't, not this morning. Got to be back by eleven.'

'What for?'

'My sister's coming home.'

'Marie? Where's she been?'

'Infirmary.'

'*Yeah?* What with?'

'Cuts, abrasions, suspected concussion.'

'No shit. What happened?'

Dennis told him. When he'd finished, Michael said, 'If your mam's fetching her in the car, why do you have to be there?'

Dennis pulled a face. 'So I'll feel bad, seeing her bandaged and all. Mam thinks it'll stop me doing lager.'

'Hooo! She could bring your Marie home in three buckets and you'd be down Thresher before the slop settled.'

'That's disgusting.'

'True though.' He looked at Dennis. 'Why'd you come? You could have phoned.'

'I had to get out for a bit, she's been giving me hell since it happened.'

'Wait till those results.'

'Aw shut *up*, can't you? It's bad enough without you reminding me.'

Michael smiled. 'You need to chill out, my friend, and I know the very thing.'

'No.'

'Whaddya *mean*, no? One little tinny, help you face the bandages.'

'No, I made a vow. I'm off it.'

'Just because your sister fell off the slide? She was going *up* it, you termite. Not your fault.'

'I know, but still . . .'

'Come *on,* Den. Ten minutes, tops. Doesn't look like Tim's coming, I'll be by myself.'

'There's the Circle.'

Michael laughed. 'When you're with the Circle you're by yourself. Come *on.*'

'Well . . .'

'Good man. First one's on me.'

'You said *one*, Michael.'

'I know, but a decent guy doesn't leave when it's his round. *Everybody* understands that, even your mam. Come on.'

Twenty-five

So Yomper follows the Welsh sergeant and everything's noisy and confused for a time, then it tails off as Bluff Cove is taken. As soon as things quieten down Yomper starts thinking about

55

his four prisoners. He thinks of them as his because they surrendered to him, but he's not sure of the rules. What the sergeant did wasn't right, couldn't be, but what about himself? Should he have protected them? Did they become his responsibility when they surrendered? Is there anything a private can do to stop a sergeant doing whatever he wants anyway?

He frets like this while the paras secure the perimeter and get billeting sorted, then requests an interview with the C.O. The Colonel will know what to do. 'What's it about?' asks Sergeant Martin, and when Yomper tells him he says, 'You don't want to go bothering the C.O. with that, lad.' 'But they'd surrendered,' goes Yomper, and Sergeant Martin says, 'Listen, lad, in the heat of battle, right, in the heat of battle it's not like other times. Snap decisions have to be made and sometimes rules get broken. That sergeant saw you hiding behind a rock with those Argies instead of moving up under fire. Maybe he thought you were chicken; saving your skin while your mates did your job for you.'

'I wasn't, sarge,' says Yomper, and Martin says, 'I'm not saying you were, lad. I'm just saying that's how it might look to somebody else. Nah.' He shakes his head. 'Forget about it, son: have a couple of pints with your mates and carry on.'

Yomper's never cared for beer but he cracks a few cans with the others and Sergeant Martin's right: he feels a lot better. Would those Argies have fretted about me, he asks himself, if it'd been the other way round? Would they thump.

Next day it's back though, worrying him. He mentions it to a couple of the lads but they don't seem bothered. Well they weren't there, were they? He lives with it for a few days, then puts in another request. This time Sergeant Martin isn't so nice about it. 'What are you, Private Dalby?' he says. 'An Argielover?' Yomper's indignant: more indignant than a private's allowed to be with a sergeant. 'It's not a matter of loving 'em sarge,' he says. 'They were human like you and me, with mums waiting for them to come home.' This cuts no ice with the sergeant, who has no mum. 'Go away, Private Dalby,' he growls, 'or you'll find yourself on a fizzer.'

So Yomper goes away. Beer helps when he can get it, but it doesn't stop him dreaming. He dreams practically every night, wakes up yelling sometimes. His mates are giving him funny looks. They stop talking when he comes in the room, ignore him on duty. When he drinks, nobody says cheers. He's acquired a nickname. Not Yomper: that comes later, when he's out of the Army. His Army nickname is Argie, same as the enemy.

Twenty-six

Mark remembered seeing a rake in one of the glass-houses and fetched it. The gravel hadn't been disturbed for some time except where vehicle tyres had pushed it into troughs and ridges, and weeds had begun to creep out from the edges. He wielded the rake, levelling the surface, uprooting weeds that he then gathered and dropped into a plastic seed tray. He started at the gate-way and moved steadily backwards towards the house.

It was hot: hotter than he'd thought. His T-shirt – Roger's T-shirt – was soon as wet as his throat was dry. He was on the point of knocking off for a minute to get himself a glass of water from the kitchen when Susan came out carrying a mug of something. Mark leaned on the rake, hoping it was whisky, knowing it wouldn't be.

'Tea. It's got milk in but no sugar.' She handed him the mug.

He grinned. 'Thanks, I don't take sugar.' Sweat trickled down his forehead. He dropped the rake, pulled a tissue out of his jeans pocket and wiped his face. 'It's like Death Valley out here.'

Susan looked at him sharply. 'Been there, have you?'

'What? Oh . . . no.' He stuffed the damp tissue in his pocket. 'Have *you*?'

'Yes, couple of years ago, part of a package.' She pulled a face. 'That heat: you could *hear* it. This is nothing.'

'I suppose not.' He sipped tea. 'This is welcome though.'

'Thought you might be ready for something.' A pause, then, 'They took us to the Manson place.'

'What's the Manson place?'

'You know: Charles Manson, the hippy murderer?'

Mark shook his head. 'Sorry, no.'

'Ah well: before your time, I suppose. He started some weird sect out in the desert but he was what they call charismatic: power to fascinate people. Rich, sophisticated people, not just hippies. He was just some young fellow they knew nothing about but they opened their beautiful homes to him, and then one day he walked in with a bunch of his disciples and murdered everybody.' Susan shivered. 'Nasty murders too: ritual killings. I've stood exactly where he stood, there in

Death Valley.' She started back to the house then turned, her sandal scrunching gravel. 'If they'd been more careful who they opened their homes to, they'd be alive today.'

Twenty-seven

'Why d'you keep coming in here? I don't like serving you and I don't think I should have to.' She was nineteen, if that.

Brasso eyeballed her. 'I've got money, you've got drink, it's your *job* to sell it.'

'You stink. Last time you peed on the floor.'

'Accident. Accidents will happen. I'll take this six-pack, bottle of Strongbow. The big 'un.'

The assistant wrinkled up her nose and served him at arm's length. Brasso parted with Michael's cash and was leaving, dangling the six-pack and with the cider under his arm, when a middle-aged woman walked in. She swerved thin-lipped round the wino and approached the counter. Brasso turned. 'Hey, love, where was you in eighty-one? Brum, right, babby in a Yourprice bag?' He shuffled over, nudged her with the six-pack. 'It's me, Mam, don't you *know* me?'

The woman flinched, edged away. 'Get away, leave me alone.'

'Yes,' snapped the shop girl, 'stop bothering the lady and get out before I call the police.'

''S OK love, I'm on my way. It's come to something though, when a lad can't say hello to his mam.' He thrust out his face and shouted, "Bye, Mam.'

'Get away from me, I'm *not* your mam.'

The girl was reaching for the telephone. Brasso turned and left.

'Hey up, Brasso!' greeted Digby as Brasso crossed Market Square. 'Saw your mam go in.' Cow and Yomper sniggered. Brasso surrendered the six-pack to Michael, sat down on the wall and twisted the cap off the bottle. 'Go on,' he growled, 'have a good laugh, see if *I* care.' He lifted the bottle to his lips, tipped back his head.

Michael jerked his head towards the park. 'C'mon, Dennis, bench in the shade.' He glanced at the thread-bare quartet on the wall. 'Catch you later, guys.' Nobody answered. They were watching Brasso, waiting for him to pass the bottle.

There were lots of people in the park and none of them had come to watch two guys demolish a six-pack, so Michael and Dennis headed for the old gazebo. Dennis was agitated, kept looking at his watch. They sat on the bench, opened a couple of cans. Michael said, 'Relax, my man, it's not yet ten fifteen. Cheers.'

'Cheers.' *I can't believe I'm here. I said I wouldn't. Promised Mam*. He raised the can, covered the hole with his lips and sucked like a greedy kisser. *Just this one, then away*.

The cold liquid ran down his throat. A warm feeling spread through his body. His agitation faded away. Some time later, two shrill kids stormed the gazebo, saw the youths, turned and fled. Dennis glanced about, looked at his watch. There were six empties on the bench and it was ten past twelve.

Twenty-eight

'Susan.' Marigold threw her car keys on the side table, took off her sun hat and patted her hair. 'You're usually gone by this time. Is something the matter?'

'No, Mrs Westhouse, I'm just off.' She dropped her work shoes in a carrier bag. 'Got talking to your young guest, put me back a bit.'

'Ah.' Marigold smiled. 'Quite the charmer, isn't he?'

'Down the cellar when I arrived, singing at the top of his voice. I nearly brained him with a bottle of gooseberries.'

'Didn't sound *that* bad, surely?'

Susan didn't smile. 'No, but *I* didn't know who he was, did I? Could've been one of those psychotic killers.'

'I *know* and I'm sorry, Susan. I should have phoned, warned you he'd be about. He's doing a wonderful job on my driveway.'

'Yes. I took him some tea out and we talked a bit. D'you know, he'd never heard of Charles Manson?'

'Well, it *was* quite a long time ago, Susan.' She smiled. 'How on earth did you get on to the subject of Manson?'

'Oh, it was Death Valley. He said the heat was like Death Valley. He's never been there though.'

Marigold nodded. 'And you *have*, and you told him about Manson's house there. I understand.'

'Yes. Well I'd best be off now if that's all right, Mrs Westhouse.'

'Of course, Susan. I'll see you tomorrow.'

'Yes,' said Susan, 'all being well.'

Mark and Marigold ate a picnic lunch on the terrace. Marigold said, 'You've made a magnificent job of the driveway, Mark. It hasn't looked so smart for years.'

Mark shrugged. 'It was nothing, Marigold. Bit of routine maintenance, that's all.'

'Ouch!'

'Oh *no*, I didn't mean . . .'

'No you're right, one *ought* to keep up to things.' She smiled. 'I understand Susan brought you tea.'

'Oh, yes.' He chuckled. 'Part of her scheme for keeping an eye on me, I believe. She thinks I'm a sinister character, you see. Suspects me of planning your ritual murder.'

'Is she right, Mark? *Are* you planning it?'

'Well, *yes*, but only as Plan B.' He grinned, helped himself to a smoked salmon and cream cheese sandwich. 'Plan A is very much nicer.'

Marigold arched her brow. '*Is* it, now? Don't you think you'd better tell me about it?'

Mark inclined his head, smiled. 'I meant to wait a day or two, give us time to get to know each other better, but since I suspect *my* Plan A is actually very like your own, I see no reason why I shouldn't reveal it now.'

'Mine?' Marigold looked puzzled. 'I don't think *I have* a Plan A, Mark: in fact I *know* I haven't.'

Mark shook his head. 'Not by that name perhaps, but you've got a plan or I wouldn't be sitting here with you now.'

His hostess shook her head. 'You've lost me I'm afraid but go on: what *is* your Plan A?'

'Nothing less than to stay here, Marigold. Permanently. It's what you want, isn't it?'

'What I . . . ?' Marigold looked at her guest. 'I assume this is some sort of joke, Mark?'

There was laughter in his eyes as he shook his head. 'No joke, Marigold. I thought it all out while you were gone, under the greengage tree, and it's perfect.' He put down his sandwich, dabbed his lips with a napkin, sat back. 'You need a man about the place, you *and* Meldilorn, and as for me, I'm strong, willing and looking for somewhere to stay.' He grinned. '*Plus* I've been half in love with you since the last time I was here. So.' His shrug spoke of their helplessness in the sweet embrace of fate.

'My God,' breathed Marigold, staring at him. 'I believe you're serious.' She'd set down her coffee cup, eased back her chair. Susan's words replayed inside her skull. '*Could've been one of those psychotic killers.*' She got up slowly, smoothly so as not to trigger Plan B, gazed down at the boy, breathing deeply to control a trembling in her limbs caused part by fury, part by fear. He returned her gaze through mocking eyes.

'Come *on*, Marigold, sit down.' He smiled. 'I may be

young but I'm not stupid. The clues were there and I picked them up, that's all.'

'Clues?' she murmured. 'What clues? What're you *talking* about?'

'Oh, come *on*. You're alone here, everybody's gone to Greece. You get a phone call from a sixteen-year-old male. You don't know him: haven't seen him since he was a kid, yet you invite him to stay. When he arrives you make a point of telling him you're divorced. He finds herbs in his room: a spray of herbs, freshly picked. When he notices the neglected state of the garden and offers to tidy it up you're all over him, big-eyed and grateful. You call him a handsome young man, mention the possibility of scandal if the village finds out he's here. You even arrange for some man to phone while you're out so he'll think he's got a rival.' He shook his head. 'You may have thought you were being subtle, Marigold: subtle enough for a sixteen-year-old anyway, but I got the message and the answer's yes, I'll stay, so sit down and drink your coffee.'

Marigold's knuckles whitened on the back of her chair. Fury shook her voice as she grated, 'How *dare* you speak to me like this. You're a boy, a *child*. How could you possibly imagine I might harbour notions . . . plans of the sort you've mentioned. It's insulting. Demeaning. It's beyond belief.' She reached across the table, knocked the napkin out of his hand and toppled his cup and saucer into his lap so that he yelped, shoved back his chair and leapt up.

'There,' she cried, 'get up and get out before I call the police!'

The coffee had been hot but not scalding. He stood clutching the wet denim with both hands, holding it away from his skin, staring at her in a wounded way that recalled to her mind the child she remembered. 'I . . . why'd you do that, Marigold? I'd never hurt you. I told you I *love* you. Are you saying you never . . . ?'

'Of *course* not.' She shook her head. 'You were a friend of my son's, that's all. I remembered a downcast little fellow, afraid of his father. I didn't invite you, you *asked* to come here. I agreed because I felt sorry for you, but I don't feel sorry now. You've abused my hospitality. There's something the matter with you. I ought to have realized that when you told me how you walked out on your exams: when you rang, probably. I suspect alcohol. Anyway I want you to go, now, without saying anything else. Go home to your parents, they're the only ones who can help you. I'll put your things in a carrier . . . don't follow me in.'

Only his eyes followed her as she crossed the terrace and entered the house. He looked stunned, still clutching the front of Roger's jeans though the coffee was cold. Inside the house the phone started ringing.

Twenty-nine

Method plus tenacity got me where I am today, Sir Ralph tells himself as he replaces the receiver and crosses another possible off the list. *Method, plus tenacity.* He'd started right after Mark's call of yesterday, compiling a list of places his son might have gone seeking refuge after walking out of school. He'd begun with relatives, of course: grandparents, aunts and uncles, cousins with their own places, then friends of the family, followed by school friends whose names he or his wife could remember Mark having mentioned. He'd ended up with a list of forty-two possibles and had called all but the last of them over the past twenty-six hours or so, to no avail. Last on the list, and a long shot if ever there was one, is a place his wife mentioned as somewhere Mark stayed with a friend one summer in his prep-school days. 'Meldilorn', she'd murmured. *He was happy there, I distinctly remember his telling me so.*

Happy. Sir Ralph frowns at the names he's scribbled down. Robert and Marigold Westhouse. *They ring no bell, which is hardly surprising since it was eight years ago and Mark has always been ready to slope off with one friend or another. Roger, this one was called. They're not in touch now. Not for years. If Mark had mentioned a Roger I'd remember. Can't stand the blasted name. Waste of a call, like all the rest. Still, method plus tenacity.* He sighs, picks up the phone, keys in some digits. Somewhere a phone starts ringing.

Thirty

'Lashford 646487, Mrs Westhouse speaking . . . No, I'm sorry, my husband can't come to the phone just now, perhaps *I* can help? . . . Oh, Sir Ralph, good afternoon . . . Yes, he *is* as a matter of fact. Since Saturday . . . No, *last* Saturday: before that he was at some inn or other in the West Country. Your son *phoned* me, Sir Ralph, sounded distressed. Asked me to let him stay for a few days. He thought my son would be here, you see: Roger. They were friends at Malsis, and Mark came to us once for part of the . . . ah, you remember . . . Yes, I can imagine how worried you must have been, you *and* Lady Penfold. That's why I insisted, as a condition of his staying here, that he phone home to let you know he was safe and well . . . Well, you know, Sir Ralph, I didn't stand over him while he *made* the call, he must have keyed in 141 to prevent its being traced . . . No, I *don't* accept that I've behaved irresponsibly . . . if I hadn't let Mark come here he'd have gone somewhere else, he certainly didn't intend coming home. In the event, things haven't gone well and he's leaving now, this minute. He'll have his rail fare, I've advised him to go home but obviously I can't guarantee he'll turn up. He's out in the garden, I'll call him if you insist but I don't know whether . . . just a tick.

'MARK? MARK, YOUR FATHER WANTS TO SPEAK TO YOU . . . MARK?

'I'm sorry, Sir Ralph. Either he hasn't heard or doesn't want to come to the phone . . . *Hold* him here? Absolutely not. Even if I could, which I doubt, it's impossible as things stand. I'd rather not go into detail, but I can't have him here a moment longer . . . There's no *point* in your driving down, Sir Ralph. As I said, he'll have money for the train, and that's the best I can do. In my opinion, your son is deeply disturbed and in need of help: I suspect alcohol . . . No I *know* you didn't ask my blasted opinion: I doubt you ever ask *anybody's*, and that might well lie at the root of your son's problem. It's a sad irony in my view that while those who supply our youngsters with other drugs go to prison, those who feed them alcohol are knighted. Goodbye, Sir Ralph.'

Thirty-one

Yomper finds himself keeping half an eye out for the Welsh sergeant, but never sees him again. A few weeks after the war ends, his unit is posted back to the UK.

He's drinking heavily by this time. A tale's gone around that he was caught hiding at Bluff Cove while his mates advanced, and nobody's talking to him. When a newspaper prints a rumour about British atrocities in the Falklands, everybody thinks Yomper's taken his story to the press. He hasn't, but he's hauled up in front of the Adjutant, who tells him it's a court-martial offence for a serviceman to talk to the newspapers. While he's about it, the Adjutant also warns him that his recent conduct and general performance has fallen below what is expected of a soldier.

It's the drinking, of course. Yomper knows this very well. What he doesn't know is how to stop.

Confused and desperate, he goes to see the Padre. *The Padre's an officer but he's a clergyman as well, and a clergyman'll care about those prisoners, won't he, that they were murdered?*

The Padre listens sympathetically, then says this to Yomper: 'In extreme circumstances a soldier, even one who is a Christian, sometimes finds himself having to choose between two evils rather than between good and evil, so he chooses what he considers to be the lesser evil. Is it better to stop fighting in order to save the lives of four enemies, or to press on and help save a thousand islanders from foreign occupation? If this was the choice that day at Bluff Cove, then who is to say the sergeant didn't make the right choice?'

Yomper can see what the Padre means, but says the sergeant's action still doesn't seem right to him.

'In that case, Private Dalby,' says the Padre, 'perhaps you ought to think about leaving the army. You can buy yourself out, you know.'

Yomper has been banking half his pay with the idea of starting his own security firm when his five years are up, but he know he'll never finish his five years now. What with the drinking and the screaming nightmares, if he doesn't leave of his own accord they'll kick him out sooner or later.

It takes every penny of his savings and a loan from his dad for Yomper to buy himself out of the army, and when he's out he can't get a job. He gets a few interviews, but when they look at his service record and see the words 'Discharge by Purchase', they put him down as a failure.

The Midborough Wine Circle don't think he's a failure, they think he's a hero. Yomper they call him, because he yomped across the soggy foggy Falklands. They can't understand why the powers–that–be let him doss down in skips instead of awarding him a medal and a pension.

Funny ideas, winos get.

Thirty-two

Hell. Mark looked down at himself. *It's like I wet my pants: have to change when she brings my kit.* Appalled by the speed with which his luck had changed, he stared at the French doors, wishing he could turn back the clock: take another crack at the last twenty minutes. He glanced at his watch. *Yeah: twenty minutes. Twenty minutes ago everything was fine. More than fine. Beautiful hostess, comfy room, lunch on the terrace: then I open my silly mouth and blow it, pouf! What the hell gets* into *me: Master of Meldilorn. Thank God I didn't say* that *out loud.*

Embarrassed to the point where it seemed impossible to face Marigold again, let alone change his clothes on her terrace, he'd half resolved to cut and run when he heard her call from indoors.

'MARK? MARK, YOUR FATHER WANTS TO SPEAK TO YOU . . . MARK?'

Father? He'd heard the phone, imagined her spilling her guts to Seward about Plan A and how she was in the middle of kicking him out, but it wasn't Seward. Somehow his father had tracked him down.

He'll come, I know he will, minute she hangs up. That does it: I'm out of here.

He strode across the terrace and round the side of the house. Marigold's Land Rover was parked just inside the gate. He broke into a jog, his trainers shushing in the gravel he'd raked. Passing the vehicle he happened to glance inside. A handbag lay on the passenger seat. On impulse he tried the door. It wasn't locked. He swung it open, reached across, grabbed the bag and trotted to the gate. There was no sign of Marigold: she was probably having to listen to his father's bloody life story. He let himself out, closing the gate behind him.

He'd no idea where he'd go. He decided not to turn right towards Lashford: that's what she'd expect him to do and either come after him in the Land Rover or tell the police. He turned left, walking rapidly between high hedges till he came to a gap and a footpath between cornfields. A few metres along this path he crouched under a hawthorn, opened the handbag and up-ended it. Among the objects that shuttered into the long grass was Marigold's pocketbook. He picked it up, hoping she carried cash. He was in luck. There was the usual Jacob's ladder of credit cards, but there were banknotes too. He extracted them, fanned them out. Five twenties, five tens and a five. He straightened up and stuffed them in a damp hip pocket of Roger's jeans, looking back along the path. Nobody was coming. He crouched, scooped everything into the handbag and hung it on the hawthorn where anybody passing by was sure to see it. This done, he strode on with no destination in mind.

Thirty-three

Dennis did some deep breathing on the way home and shook his head a lot, but everything still seemed muzzy. He decided to call in at the newsagent's for a tube of strong mints. It would give him a chance to practise talking clearly and the mint might take the lager off his breath. As he neared Peartree Gardens with four mints bulging his cheeks, he rehearsed the story he'd made up to tell his mother.

We were in the park, right, me and Michael, looking at the ducks on the pond and we heard a little kid crying. It was coming from behind the boathouse. We went and looked and there was this girl, five or six years old, crying her eyes out. We asked her what the matter was and she didn't know. So we said, 'Who brought you to the park?' and she said, 'Mummy.' So we said, 'Let's go see if we can find Mummy then.' And she stopped crying and, like, toddled along between us, holding our hands. We knew her mam'd be looking for her so what we did was we headed for that big open space between the playground and the bowling greens. People can see you a mile off there 'cause there's no trees or bushes. So we walked her across it a couple of times and, sure enough, this woman comes hurrying towards us looking wild. You can see she's been crying. She's, like, 'Thank God, oh thank God', down on her knees hugging the kid. So me and Michael just walk off and I look at my watch and it's ten past twelve.

It was a plausible story, *and* it'd prove he wasn't irresponsible where little kids are concerned, if only he could manage to tell it without slurring his words.

Turned out to be so much wasted effort though because, when he reached number 44, both doors were locked. The Micra was parked at the kerb so he knew they were back from the infirmary, but nobody came when he knocked and when he tried peering through the windows he couldn't see anything for the nets.

'Mam!' He rattled the letter slot. 'Let me in, Mam, I couldn't help it. We found this kid in the park . . .' It sounded unconvincing, shouted through the slot. It was the sort of story you need to tell face to face. After a bit, nosy Mr Atkinson looked out to see what all the noise was about, so Dennis stopped kicking the door and sat on the step. He didn't believe his mother would leave him locked out for ever, but all the same it wasn't fair. He was due at work at six and he'd need to get ready, and it was rotten of her to treat him like this when all he'd done was restore a lost child to its mam.

Thirty-four

After what felt like a couple of miles he came to a road. The footpath continued on the far side but the day was oppressively hot and Mark's mouth felt dry. If he followed the road there was a fair chance he'd come to a village with a pub. He turned right and walked on, skipping sideways now and then to avoid oozes of molten tar.

He'd picked the wrong direction. If he'd turned left he'd have walked into Apton Magna round the first bend. If he'd *looked* he'd have spotted the church tower in its clump of ancient yews. As it was, he walked eight and a half miles, dodging tar and watching traffic in case one of the approaching vehicles turned out to be Sir Ralph's BMW. Roger's T-shirt was plastered across his shoulders and the soles of his feet burned in his own expensive trainers. When he plodded into Lithgow it was seven o'clock and he'd been walking for three and three-quarter hours.

Lithgow's pub was the Chequered Skipper. 'Penfold', it said on the board. Mark fished out Marigold's wad, peeled off the five and went in. It was cool inside, and dim after the relentless glare. There was a flat, beery smell that started his mouth watering. He approached the bar.

'Pint of bitter, please.' The landlord, a broad man with a red face behind an extravagant yellow moustache, glared at him through pale blue button eyes. 'Eighteen, I suppose?'

'Nineteen.'

'Aye, and I'm Little Red Riding Hood. Coke do you? It's cold.'

'My name's Penfold, my father owns the brewery and I want bitter.'

'Listen, sonny.' The landlord laid his thick arms flat on the bar, leaned over and spoke quietly. 'Your name could be Rumpelstiltskin, your father might own a troupe of dancing mammoths and you could want a bathful of banana-flavoured ice-cream, and it'd *still* be Coke you'd get in my pub. Now, d'you want it or don't you? Makes no odds to me.'

Mark avoided the man's eyes, nodded. 'All right.' *Should he tell him to stuff it, walk out but then what? How far's the next village?* He must take the weight off his feet, drink something cold. He had the place to himself so at least nobody had witnessed his defeat. He carried the glass to a table by the empty fireplace and sat down.

The cold sweet liquid felt good in his gullet. He resisted the temptation to guzzle, spinning out the pleasurable business of quenching his thirst. He'd entered the Chequered Skipper with the vague intention of having a drink and a rest then moving on, but now that his most urgent needs had been met three things dawned on him: he was hungry, his feet couldn't possibly carry him much further tonight and it was getting late. There was a menu on the table. He resented the idea of putting more business the landlord's way but could see no sensible alternative. People had started coming in: a few old men, a younger chap from upstairs who might be a company rep. One old man glared so pointedly in Mark's direction while his pint was being pulled that he knew he'd pinched his customary spot. Mark waited till the landlord wasn't serving, then walked across to the bar.

'Yes?'

'I'd like a ham sandwich please, and have you a room free?'

'Room yes, free no: cost you eighteen for the night, continental breakfast. Where's your bag?'

'There isn't a bag: I travel light.'

'What about a wallet?' A grandad chuckled, further down the bar.

Mark flushed. 'I have the money, d'you want it in advance?' He produced the notes.

'I reckon that's best, don't you?'

Mark handed over a twenty. The landlord nodded. 'Room eighteen, sandwich two: just right unless you want another Coke.'

'Yes, I'd like another.'

'One-o-nine then.' Mark counted out the coins, stacked them on the bar.

'Ta. Sandwich'll be a few minutes, rooms're up there, you're in number two.' He gazed at Mark. 'Not on the *run*, are we?'

Mark felt a stab of anger, reddened. 'No we're *not*.' He ached to say more but bit his tongue. The fellow would probably welcome an excuse to kick him out and keep the money.

He took his Coke, turned. The gimmer who'd glared had bagged his table.

Thirty-five

It was twenty to six when Dennis's mother unlocked the door. Twenty to rotten six. 'You've made me late for work, Mam,' he whined.

'Give you time to sober up,' she snapped, 'and your sister's all right, thanks for asking.'

'I was *going* to ask, and I don't know what you mean, *sober up*. Me and Michael found this kid in the park . . .'

'Yes, I know. Your dad found her a time or two as well, and *he* used to celebrate with strong mints. Must be in the genes.'

He was eight minutes late at Wicklow's. Packers work in teams of three. The more orders a team packs, the more it earns. Viv and Ernest weren't happy. Ernest made a big thing out of looking at his watch. 'Eight minutes, Dennis. Two, three orders adrift.'

'Second time this week,' put in Viv.

Dennis eyeballed her. 'It's Monday. How the heck can it be second time this week?' *Daft cow.*

'Second time in the last few days, I mean. Rodgers noticed.'

'Thanks, guys.' He shrugged into his overall. 'Covering for me, I mean.'

'You can't *cover* for someone on a team job,' growled Ernest. 'You want to get your act together, lad, instead of blaming other folk.'

Rodgers appeared, dodging between hurrying packers. 'Word with you, Dennis. My office.'

The supervisor's office was a glass cubicle in the middle of the warehouse. Sitting in it like a spider in its web, Rodgers was able to watch everything that went on. Dennis muttered a bad word and followed the lanky, balding supervisor across the busy floor.

'Now then, lad.' Rodgers flopped into his swivel

chair and gazed up at Dennis. 'What d'you think you're playing at, eh?'

Dennis hadn't eaten since breakfast. The warehouse was overheated and he felt dizzy. He shook his head. 'I don't know what you mean, Mr Rodgers.'

'Don't you? What time is it?'

There was a digital clock on one glass wall. Dennis glanced at it. 'Ten past six.'

'Exactly, and what time does the evening shift start?'

'Six.'

'Six, and you come strolling in at eight minutes past like Lord Muck. Last Thursday you condescended to join us at eighteen-fourteen. I know because I wrote it down.' He shook his head. 'That's twenty-two minutes, lad. Twenty-two minutes belonging to Wicklow's that you've stolen.'

'Not *stolen*.' Anger flared in Dennis. 'You don't pay us till we start, whatever time it is.'

'DON'T TALK BACK!' The high-pitched bark made Dennis flinch. Rodgers had half-risen in his seat, now he sank back and growled, 'I didn't bring you in here to discuss terms and conditions like a flipping shop-steward. You're here to get a warning. A *final* warning.'

'But it's the first time . . .'

'A FINAL warning.' The supervisor looked at him through narrowed eyes. 'You've a smart mouth on you, lad, but the rest of you's not so clever. I know what your trouble is: I've two lads of my own. It's the lager. Clubbing, and the lager, so listen. Get a grip of yourself. Have some early nights. Think about other people, not just yourself – Viv and Ernest and, if not them, your mother. Your mother didn't bring you up so you could chuck your life away, boozing and boogying or whatever you call it, so pull yourself together because there's plenty of kids out there waiting for your job. Understand what I'm saying?'

Dennis nodded, which hurt because his head had started to ache. 'Yes, Mr Rodgers.' *I was going to ask about more hours, can't now. Got to get a grip.* Got *to.*

'All right, Dennis, apologize to your team-mates and work like hell and remember: I've got my eye on you.'

Thirty-six

Where next? The question haunted Mark's night, and he came down prickly eyed to a breakfast about as continental as Easter Island. He considered dunking the single stale roll in the watery instant, but a lump'd probably drop off and he'd be left with bread soup. The company rep came down and was insensitive enough to ignore five vacant tables and join him with a perfunctory, 'D'you mind?'

He was a talker of course. 'Mike Trafford: mobile phones. You?'

'School hols. Walking.' *Sod off.*

'Lucky man. Heading for . . . ?'

Mark shrugged. 'Dunno, actually.' It was the truth.

'I see: footloose and fancy free. Well, if I were in your shoes I'd head for Spaxton Market, definitely.'

'Shopping?'

'Lord, *no*. It's a village, Spaxton Market. Famous. Surprised you haven't heard of it.'

Mark shrugged again.

'Check it out, squire, you'll never regret it. It's on the old Pilgrim's Way. Lovely Saxon church, holy well, green with duckpond: sort of spot they put on picture postcards. *And —*' pause for effect — 'by a strange coincidence I'm going in that general direction myself. Happy to give you a lift.'

'Oh no.' *Sounds rude, didn't mean* . . . 'I'm walking, you see. Prefer it.' He laid a palm on his stomach. Car sick.'

'Ah.' The rep wheeled out his understanding bit. 'Got a cousin like that. Awful thing. Still.' He brightened, indicated an adjacent window. 'Perfect day for it. Six miles, give or take. There for lunch, no danger.'

'Right.' Mark drained his coffee cup, smiled. 'Might as well make a start. Thanks for the info.'

'You're wecome, uh . . . ?'

'Seward. Charles Seward.'

'Good meeting you, Charles. Probably pass you along the road, give you a toot.'

'I'll listen out.'

The landlord was wiping tables in the bar. Mark said 'Bye' in passing and he didn't even look up.

Thirty-seven

Leaving Wicklow's at nine, Dennis was surprised to find Tim waiting for him just beyond the security hut. 'Hey up, Tim.'

'Hi.' Tim smiled wanly. 'I thought I'd wait by the fountain, look at the fishes, but that miserable sod wouldn't let me past.'

'Oooh, *no* chance!' Dennis shook his head. 'They're *mad* on security, Wicklow's. If you've got a bag, *any* sort of bag, they search it when you're leaving. That's why I never carry one.'

'Scared the workers'll nick the stock, eh?'

'Absolutely.' Dennis grinned. 'This one *would*, and all.' He looked at his friend. 'What's up anyway?'

'Dosh. I was wondering if you could lend me a bit, just till I get paid.' Tim helped with a milk round and did odd jobs at weekends on a chicken farm.

Dennis pulled a face. 'You're *joking*, aren't you? You know *I* never have anything. Takes me all my time to stretch Friday to Friday. Won't Dempsey give you a sub?'

Tim shook his head. 'A sub's no good, Dennis. I need eighty.'

'Eighty *quid*? What the heck for – deposit on a world cruise?'

'No, I owe it.'

'You owe eighty smackers? Who *to*, for Pete's sake?'

'Donny Conway.'

'What?' Dennis stopped dead, gazed at his friend. 'You haven't been borrowing dosh from *that* crook.'

'Only once, Den. I *had* to: I'd taken some of my dad's club money. You know, the dosh he looks after for the bowls club? It was only twenty, so I could go to Hackers. I meant to put it back out of my wage but I spent it when I was rat-arsed. I knew my dad might find out any minute and I didn't know what to do so I went to see Donny, borrowed the twenty.'

'You said eighty.'

'Yeah, it's eighty now because of the interest. Every week you don't pay, it doubles. I borrowed it two weeks ago. On Friday it'll be three weeks.'

'And you'll owe *a hundred and sixty*?'

'That's right.'

'Guy ought to be in jail.'

'I know, but he isn't, and that's why I've got to get dosh. If it gets to one-sixty I've *no* chance.'

'Yeah, but like, what *happens*? I mean one-sixty, three-twenty, six-forty: *nobody* could find that. What does he *do* when it reaches, say, twelve-eighty?'

'You *know* what he does, Den. *Everyone* knows. He sends his minders after you and you're found up an alley with two broken legs, and that's if you're lucky. If they get carried away you wind up dead.'

'Shit, and I thought *I* had problems.' Dennis kicked a pebble. 'I don't know what to *say*, Timmo. Eighty quid in four days doesn't seem possible.'

'Junkies manage it *every day*.'

'Oh yeah, but they mug people, break into houses, cars. *You* can't . . .'

'I haven't ruled it out, Den: I *can't*. I *like* my legs. I'm scared. You've got to help me.'

'Yeah.' Dennis nodded. 'I *want* to help, I really do, but *Donny Conway*.' He pulled a face. 'Donny Conway's a *biggie*, Timmo. A *biggie*.'

Thirty-eight

Mark stood in the shadow of the Chequered Skipper, glancing up and down the road. It was only eight o'clock, but polarization puddles on the tarmac promised another hot day. He'd a hundred and thirty-two pounds of Marigold's money left: enough for a few days, but then what?

'*Go home to your parents, Mark. Go today.*' *Easy for you to say, Marigold. It'll come to that in the end, I know, but I'm not ready so it's Spaxton Market, then we'll see.*

It was another sticky hike. As Mark walked he found himself fantasizing about Marigold's fragrant coffee, Marigold's Glayva: about Marigold. He kept an eye out for the Land Rover, and for his father's car, though why Sir Ralph would drive along this particular road he'd no idea. The tar was melting again and the soles of his feet felt as though they were on fire. He'd gone perhaps a mile when a silver Mondeo pulled up and Mike Trafford stuck his head out. 'Want to change your mind about that lift, Charles? Cooler in here.'

Mark shook his head. 'I'd probably throw up over the upholstery and you wouldn't want that. Thanks, though.'

'Suit yourself, squire. By the way, I put up at the Tap and Spile when I'm staying in Spaxton Market. Nice little place, you might want to give it a go.'

'Thanks, I'll look out for it.'

'Cheers then.'

'Bye.'

Heat warped the Mondeo's shape as it sped away. Mark took off his jacket, mopped his forehead with it and knotted the sleeves round his waist. Sweat plastered Roger's T-shirt to his back and he remembered a film he'd watched on TV about some chaps crossing the Western Desert in an old ambulance during the Second World War. It was an ancient film, black and white, but there was a bit where one of the characters described the drink he'd have when they reached Alexandria. Lager in a tall glass, so cool that beads of condensation would form on the outside of the glass and run down. Mark could *see* that glass, and not in black and white either. He groaned and plodded on.

It was nearly half eleven when he saw the square tower of a church thrusting through treetops ahead. A minute later he came to a milestone on a plinth set into a neatly shorn verge. A plate on the stone read simply SPAXTON MARKET. Graceful trees rose out of neat gardens to overhang the road, their shade soothing Mark's eyes after the glare. Reaching what he assumed was the centre of the village, he collapsed on to a wooden bench overlooking a long green pond with ducks, willows and a dense border of flags whose yellow heads were reflected in the water.

That loud rep was right, he thought. *This is gorgeous: especially that bit over there.* He was gazing at a dazzlingly white building beyond the pond. It stood in the middle of a row of shops in weathered brick, and a board on its creeper-veined wall told him he was looking at the Tap and Spile.

Thirty-nine

Dennis raised himself up on one elbow and squinted at the clock on his bedside unit. 01.12. He flopped back with a groan. *Two hours I've been lying here, not a minute's kip. If I could just, like, empty my mind, then shut it with all the thoughts outside like the bouncers shutting Hackers for the night. Dark and quiet, after all the glare and noise.*

There were three subjects, and it was like they were pounding round a race track that went in one ear, curved across his brain, out through the other ear and round again. They must have done about a thousand laps already and nobody was dropping back.

In front with a narrow lead was Tim. He was Dennis's best mate and he desperately wanted to help him, but no matter how hard he tried he couldn't think of a way. Behind Tim ran Donny Conway and two minders. No wonder he was leading.

After Tim and his pursuers came Dennis's mam. She looked worn out but daren't slacken off because Dennis's results were closing fast and she dreaded what she'd see when they lapped her. Dennis could see them: a straggle of Ds and Fs running hard, intent on breaking his mother's heart.

Last came Dennis himself, hard-pressed by a shapeless rolling tangle representing confusion, rejection and failure. It moved surprisingly fast for such a shaggy thing, and only frequent swigs of lager kept him running. Trouble was he had to pause each time so it seemed he was doomed to be caught.

At 01. 14 Dennis's mind dipped to standby mode and his thoughts ran on as dreams. Dennis was asleep and didn't notice the difference.

Forty

Mark sat watching the ducks till his thirst was greater than his tiredness, then got up and strolled round the pond and across the cobbled street to the Tap and Spile, seeing in his mind that glass with the condensation. He'd just got through the door when he heard angry voices and two men came lurching through a doorway on his left, shoving between them a third man who was obviously reluctant to leave. Mark flattened himself against the wall to let them pass. As the trio drew level the one in the middle noticed him and shouted, 'You don't wanna bother with this dump, son: no appreciation of a fella's custom.' The other two manhandled him to the door, propelled him into the brightness outside and came back up the hallway, scowling and rubbing their hands together. Mark followed them into what turned out to be a long cool room with beams, coppertop tables and bar. One of the men went behind the bar, the other to the half-full tankard he'd obviously left to go to the landlord's assistance. There was nobody else in the place.

Mark stood at the gleaming counter. The landlord rinsed his hands at the sink, dried them on a bar towel and shot an inquiring look at his new customer. 'Pint of lager, please,' said Mark, in what he hoped was a matter-of-fact voice.

'Foster's or Stella?'

'Oh ah, F-F-Foster's I think. Yes, Foster's.' He was so surprised at finding himself unchallenged he nearly blew it. The landlord smiled to himself as he drew the pint and set it on a mat in front of the boy. 'Two seventeen, lad. Come far, have you?'

Mark handed over a ten. 'Not far really: Lashford.' He took a pull of the lager. *Ice Cold in Alex, name of that film.*

The landlord slid his change across. 'Driving?'

'N-no, walking. Walking holiday.'

'Phew!' The man shook his head. 'Rather you than me, this weather.' He glanced along the bar. 'What do *you* say, Raymond?'

Raymond pulled a face. 'You know me, Ivor: walk nowhere if I can help it.'

Emboldened by his apparent acceptance, Mark jerked his head towards the door. 'Spot of bother just now?'

'Oh aye.' The landlord nodded. 'Amazing some of the types we get out here nowadays. Never used to.'

'I blame TV,' growled Raymond. 'They see some flaky mock-up on the box, s'posed to be a cosy country pub full of amiable locals going *gorr* and *arr* and playing shove-halfpenny, and they come expecting to see the real thing. Plonkers.'

'Yeah,' agreed the landlord, 'you get their sort, but that fella wasn't one of 'em. Deadbeat, he was: alkie from Midborough or somewhere, scratching and muttering and scrabbling through his small change. Beats me how he found his way here: no bus today, nor yesterday come to that.'

'Must've walked,' suggested Raymond, 'like our young friend here.'

Mark grinned. 'Didn't see him on the road.' He drained his tankard, pushed it across the counter. 'Same again please, and I'd like a room for a night or two if you're not full?'

The landlord took the tankard, gave the boy a speculative look. '*I'm* not full, son, but I reckon you are. Settle for half, eh? Half, bite to eat and a room, how's that?'

Raymond chuckled into his beer. Mark smiled, shrugged. He was feeling pretty woozy: probably the heat. 'OK. I'd like a ham sandwich, a half of that and a room.'

The man nodded. 'Where's your bag?'

'No bag: travelling light.'

'Ah: like in the song, eh?'

Mark frowned. 'Song?'

'Never mind. I assume you've got the necessary?'

'Money? Oh, yes.' He sported his wad. 'I could pay now if you like.'

'No, no, later'll be fine, but I'll give you a word of advice: don't flash it about like that or you won't have it long. Like I said, there's some funny folk these days, even in Spaxton Market.'

FORTY-ONE

'Why don't we run it by the Circle,' suggested Michael, 'see if *they* come up with anything?'

A persistent drizzle was falling on the park, keeping it largely deserted, making distant objects fuzzy. The three friends were in the old gazebo, sharing the bench with a six-pack they'd clubbed together to buy.

Tim scoffed. 'Only thing the Circle ever comes up with is sitting on that wall like a line of flipping crows, swearing and spitting.'

'You don't know,' put in Dennis. 'They've been around, those guys. Experience. It's worth a try, we're getting nowhere by ourselves.'

Tim shrugged. 'Try 'em if you want, it'll do no good.' His eyes filled with tears. 'Nothing will.' He turned his face away, ripped the tab off a can and swigged.

It was just after eleven when the three reached Market Square. They were broke, but they'd saved a couple of cans. Michael handed one to Yomper, one to

Cow. Cow looked at his and whined, 'This *all*, man? Me here from seven o'clock, waitin'.'

'Half that's for Digby,' growled Michael, 'we've troubles of our own.'

Yomper drank, passed his can to Brasso, scowled up at Michael. 'What troubles?'

'The usual.' Michael sat down. 'Dosh.'

'That en't *trouble*s.' Yomper belched loudly enough to turn a few heads. 'Everybody got *that* problem. You had *my* dreams, y'd know about troubles.'

Michael shook his head. 'We're not just broke, my man: we *owe*.'

'*Weowe*,' mimicked Yomper. 'Sound like a bleedin' moggy, lad. *Everybody* owes: it's how people live today.'

'They don't owe Donny Conway.'

The drunk's mouth fell open, revealing greenish teeth. 'You owe *Donny*? How much?'

'More'n *you*'ve got, my man.'

'I said how much?'

'One-sixty come Saturday. Gonna *lend* us it, are you?'

Yomper shook his greasy locks. 'Wish I could though. I seen . . .'

'What?' Michael waited. '*What?*'

'Nothing. Seen nothing.'

'Come *on*, Yomper, you started to say something, what was it?'

'I uh . . .' Yomper snatched the can out of Brasso's fist, sucked greedily, wiped his mouth with the back of his hand. 'Place I kip in. Alleyway. Donny's men bring guys there. In a car, no lights. I hear screams, other noises. Seen 'em crawl off after, them that can.'

'And you don't *do* anything: to help 'em, I mean?'

Yomper shook his head again. 'You're joking. Old paras, see? Top someone like me, think they was doing me a favour. No. I keep my head down, mind my own business.'

''Scuse me?' Brasso leaned across Yomper, looked at Michael. 'This Donny. Bothering you, is he?'

'Bothering *me*,' said Tim, who hadn't sat down.

Brasso nodded. 'Same difference.' He plucked the can from Yomper's hand, threw back his head and drank till it was empty. He regarded Tim through narrowed eyes. 'I know a way to fix moneylenders, done it before.'

'You *have*?' said Tim, eagerly. 'How?'

The drunk patted the wall beside him. 'Come, sit down and I'll tell you.'

Forty-two

He ate his sandwich, finished his half of lager and had a look at the room he'd taken for two nights. He liked the Tap and Spile and would have booked three nights, but at thirty-five pounds a night his funds would have been dangerously stretched. As it was he was left with forty-eight pounds eighty-two and he knew deep down he'd be forced to start making his way home on Thursday or face destitution on the streets.

For the moment though he was pleasantly tipsy among friendly people in the most picturesque village he'd ever seen, the sun was shining and he was determined to enjoy every minute of it. He left the inn and made his way towards the bench he'd rested on earlier. Two old men nipped in just ahead of him so he lay on the grass with his hands under his head and fantasized wistfully about Marigold till the sun cast the shadow of an ancient horse-chestnut tree across the bench and the old men left. He took possession of the seat and watched a laughing toddler tear chunks off a loaf and throw them to the ducks. Her throw was a looping approximation and many pieces fell short of the water. When her mother led the child away, some ducks came ashore and were waddling towards the food when a man appeared, waving his arms and making shooing noises. Mark recognized the fellow he'd seen thrown out of the Tap and Spile. While the ducks milled and quacked at the water's edge the man scuttled about, gathering pieces of bread, which he dropped into the pockets of his threadbare jacket. One or two passers-by noticed and stopped to watch, but nobody said anything. When he'd got all the big pieces, the man hurried off the way he'd come, leaving the ducks to hoover up the crumbs.

By the time the sun cleared the horse-chestnut, it was a smoky orange ball above the pantiles opposite. Mark watched it dip below the roofs then got up and, pleasantly tired, strolled back to the inn and his bed.

Forty-three

Donny Conway has dosh coming out of his ears but he's a tight-fisted wassock so he always eats breakfast at the Italia. The Italia's famous for its gigantic portions and small bills, and it's open seven days a week. Donny doesn't eat alone: he doesn't do anything alone. Too many people hate him, all of them with good reason. Donny takes a table for four and his heavies sit round him watching the other customers, daring anyone to so much as glance in Donny's direction.

Ten o'clock Wednesday morning. Donny and the minders at their usual table, tucking away the eggs and bacon, the beans and sausage, the bread and coffee. Apart from them and two postmen at another table, the place is empty. The door opens and a clergyman comes in. The minders give him a brief glance and chomp on. Priests are the only people who pose no potential threat to their boss.

Instead of bagging a table or ordering at the hatch, the clergyman approaches the ugly quartet, hooks a chair from an adjacent table and joins them with a mild 'Excuse me, I hope you don't mind?'

Close up he's a thin, scruffy-looking specimen with a bad haircut and a grubby dog-collar. The minders stare at him in silence, chewing in his face. Donny puts down his knife and fork. A nerve twitches at the corner of his right eye. When his mouth is empty he murmurs, 'Yes?'

'You won't know me,' says the priest. 'My name's Nicholas Cribb, and I'm assistant to the Reverend Paul Sampson.' He twinkles. 'No doubt you're familiar with Paul's name for lo: it appeareth in the local press thrice weekly.' If this is a joke it makes no impression on Donny or his minders, who stare impassively and say nothing. Unabashed, Cribb continues. 'Well, it's on Paul's behalf that I'm here this morning. You've probably read about the drop-in centre he operates in the church hall at St Michael's?'

This time he waits for a response. Donny's eggs are getting cold. 'Yes,' he snaps, 'what about it?'

'This about it,' says the priest mildly. 'Paul is doing splendid work with young people who have become dependent on drugs or alcohol. That's why he gets such a good press.'

'Look, reverend,' sighs Donny, 'if it's money you're after you're wasting your breath; I don't make donations.'

'He don't like guys who ask for donations,' growls the nearest minder, 'even reverends.'

''Specially if they reverends,' says another.

Cribb shakes his head. 'I'm not seeking a donation, Mr Conway, not directly anyway.'

Donny scowls. 'Whaddya mean, not directly?'

'I'll come straight to the point,' says the priest. 'There's a lad on Paul's programme: name of Broadbent. Tim Broadbent. He's alcoholic, or on the way to becoming so. He dropped in a day or two ago, pleading for help. That's unusual, you know: most youngsters

94

deny they've got a problem. Paul has a good feeling about this lad: believes he can pull him round, but there's one thing in the way.'

Donny sighs again. 'And what's that?'

'Debt. The young man was desperate enough recently to borrow a small sum of money in order to buy drink. He borrowed it from you.'

'No.' Donny shakes his head, drops his voice. 'Not from me, reverend. Neither a lender nor a borrower be, that's my motto.' He glances shiftily around the café. 'You got the wrong guy.'

'Rubbish, man!' The priest eyeballs the moneylender. 'Everybody in Midborough knows what you do. Listen,' he leans in and murmurs, 'I'm not here to judge you: that's for a higher power. I'm here to beg a favour, that's all. A small favour.'

'Ha!' sneers Donny. 'Don't tell me: you want I should write it off, right?'

The priest nods. 'That's all, Mr Conway.'

'All?' Donny yells, then remembers where he is and lowers his voice. 'Have you any idea what it'd do to my business if I let this kid off and it got out?'

The clergyman nods. 'I can see it might dent your reputation for . . . er . . . ruthlessness, but I imagine it'd be far more damaging to you if the press found out you'd deliberately sabotaged my colleague's attempt to redeem this poor boy: and of course there's the matter of your immortal soul.'

'My immortal bleedin' soul,' mutters Donny. One of the minders laughs and cracks his knuckles. The clergyman nods. 'That's approximately what I said, Mr

Conway. You have my word as a priest that if you can see your way to granting this favour, nobody will learn about it from me or anybody connected with St Michael's.'

'Ha.' The moneylender stares at his congealed eggs. The minders stare at the priest. The priest stares at the floor. The postmen leave. The waitress comes and clears the vacated table. Donny picks up his fork and jabs it into an egg. 'Yeah, OK.'

'Bless you, Mr Conway.' The priest stands, offers his hand. Donny looks up at him. 'This time only. Understand?'

The priest nods. 'Of course.' They shake hands. The clergyman leaves.

Donny shoves his plate away, glares at a minder. 'Fresh coffee. Now.'

Forty-four

Thirty-five pounds isn't cheap for a room, but the Tap and Spile threw in a breakfast that'd choke a hippo. Sunlight fell in squares on the carpet as Mark polished off a bowl of cornflakes, a plate of sausage, eggs and bacon and a rack of toast with butter and tangy marmalade. There were three people at breakfast besides himself but nobody joined him, which was good. He drained his coffee cup, dabbed his lips and went outside.

Another glorious morning. Mike Trafford had

mentioned the church and a holy well. Mark decided to check them out. He could see the church tower so he'd do that, then ask somebody about the well.

The church stood among gnarled yews, its grey stones dappled with sunlight, moss and lichen. He walked all round the outside before going into the porch. There was a thick door with iron studs. He pulled it open and peered into the gloom, hoping he'd got the place to himself.

There seemed to be nobody about. A folding table just inside held a stack of printed guides and a placard with *20p each* on it. A safe or poor-box built into the wall had a slot for coins. A card taped under the slot informed visitors that the box was emptied daily. Mark fished a twenty out of his pocket, pushed it through the slot and took a guide. He was squinting at the first page, holding it at an angle to get light from a small window when a voice behind him growled, 'Can you credit it, eh?'

He started, turned and saw the man who'd beaten the ducks to their supper. 'Hell's bells,' he croaked, 'you scared me half to death. Credit *what*?'

'Sorry, lad, been here all night. *That.*' He nodded at the card. 'Emptied daily. Wouldn't you think the *church'd* trust people enough to leave its miserable twenty-pees ungathered for a day or two?'

Mark shrugged. 'I dunno, I suppose they must've had thefts or something. I mean, churches were never locked at one time, but they lock 'em now. At night, I mean.' He looked at the man. 'Don't they lock *this* one?'

'Oh, aye.'

'But didn't you just say you'd been here all night?'

'Yes.'

'So how . . . ?'

The fellow chuckled. 'Easy. There's one of them tomb things over there: you know, fella laid out on top. Well, it's dark in that corner, even in the daytime. All I did was get down behind the tomb when the verger or whoever came to lock up for the night. He had a quick walk round, looked in the pews but it wasn't much of a search. It never is. I've spent some comfy nights in churches.' He chuckled. 'Scared a few flower ladies and all, first thing of a morning. And they don't *all* empty the poor-box daily.'

Mark looked at him. 'You don't . . . ?'

'I do. Why not? It's for the poor, and *I'm* poor. Think of it as cutting out the middle man.'

Mark smiled, he couldn't help it. 'Nothing doing here though, eh?'

'Oh, I wouldn't say that. Good drop of wine with my supper, nice dry kip. Only thing missing's breakfast, and I was wondering if *you* might . . .'

'*Me?*' Mark shook his head. 'I've nothing to spare, sorry.'

'You're at the Tap and Spile, that's not cheap. *And* you talk posh. I bet Daddy's loaded.'

Mark nodded. 'You got that right, but it isn't doing me any good. In fact I'm on the run from my father.'

The man grinned. 'Funny: *I'm* on the run from my kids. Where you going?'

'I'm not sure. I might head for Midborough tomorrow.'

'I used to live there, it's a dump.'

'Well, I haven't decided yet. I'm off to find the holy well now. Goodbye.'

'See you later . . . er?'

'Charles.'

The man nodded. 'I'm Jim. Catch you later, Charles.'

Forty-five

Cow and Digby followed Brasso into the market hall lavatories to get their kit back. Cow's dark jacket, Digby's kecks. The boys waited outside with Yomper. Tim fidgeted, biting his lip. Yomper looked at him. 'Calm down, for Pete's sake, it'll be all right.'

Two minutes and the three emerged wearing their own clothes. Tim confronted Brasso. 'How'd it go, Brasso? Did he . . .?'

'*Course* he did.' Brasso grinned. 'I *told* you you could count on your Uncle Stephen, didn't I?'

'Yeah you did, but . . .' Impulsively, Tim threw his arms round the drunk. '*Thanks*, Brasso, you saved my life. I never thought it'd work and I can't *ever* thank you enough.'

'Oi, steady *on*.' People were staring. Brasso wriggled out of the hug. 'You *can* thank me enough; bottle of Strongbow'll do it, only *don't* borrow from Donny to

99

buy it.' The others laughed. People were still looking so they left the market for their customary bit of wall.

'Come *on*, Reverend Brasso,' urged Cow, when they were seated, 'tell all o' we the parable of the Priest and the Money Lender.'

More laughter. Tim leaned forward to look at Brasso. 'I . . . I'm broke, Brasso. We all are, but I won't forget that bottle. As soon as . . .'

''S OK, lad.' Brasso nodded. 'I know you won't forget.'

'No, but, like, I feel *rotten*, y'know? I mean, you risked your life, and I can't even . . .'

'Don't worry.' The drunk shook his head. 'It was no big deal.' He grinned. 'Fact is, I *like* being someone else now and then. Makes a change.'

'You mean you've done stuff like it *before*?' This from Dennis.

Brasso nodded. 'Oh aye, *hundreds* of times. I'm Major Henshaw, y'know; Brigade of Guards, retired.' The cut-glass accent was flawless. 'That was when my clobber was in better nick, of course. I'm Lars Pedersen, the Danish hiker who's dosh has been . . . how you say . . . pinchet, and I'm need ten pounds the ticket for the train to buy. *Aaand* I'm . . . let's see . . . oh yes, Ernest Lawson the heartless landlord, insisting on three months' rent in advance on a flat I'm letting, which is really a council flat only the poor bleedin' tenent don't find that out till old Ernie's long gone, *and* the three months' rent. And then of course I'm the Reverend Nicholas Cribb, doing God's work by collecting on behalf of poor Romanian orphans, but *really* on behalf of Stephen King, who's gagging for a few swift bevvies.'

'Stephen *King*?' Michael looked at Brasso. 'Like the writer? That your real name, is it?'

Brasso shrugged. 'Reallest one I've got. They called me Stephen in care; no second name. I picked King 'cause I like his books. It'll have to do till I find my mum, ask her what *she* called me.'

Cow chuckled. '*Know* what she call you, man: she call you "Oh shit what I suppose to do wit *this* ting?"'

Everybody laughed. Well no, not everybody. Brasso stared morosely at the ground till they'd finished, then said, 'D'you *wanna* hear this bleedin' parable or not?'

They did.

Forty-six

The holy well turned out to be a sort of trough in the thickness of an old wall down Holywell Lane, and it was dry. Mark wasn't bothered: he didn't care for all this heritage stuff anyway. It was a matter of passing the time, that's all: trying not to think about going home, though he knew he'd have to soon.

As he sauntered about the village he found himself watching for Jim. '*Catch you later, Charles.*' He didn't want to be caught by Jim. With forty-eight pounds for food and fares he couldn't afford to subsidize the guy. Also, Jim was obviously a drunk and Mark was afraid the man would persuade him to invest in a bottle of something. He knew from the disaster at Meldilorn that once he started drinking anything might happen, and from his thirst that he wouldn't need much persuading. He looked in shop windows, wondering vaguely about the possibility of getting some sort of job here, a cheap room.

At lunchtime he bought a meat pie and sat on the green to eat it. He'd have liked to lie down afterwards with the sun on his face but, if he did, Jim might sneak up on him, so instead he walked about looking for *'Staff wanted'* notices. He didn't find any.

Spaxton Market was a small place, and by early afternoon Mark was bored. There'd been no sign of the drunk – maybe he'd left the village. There was a phone box by the green. On impulse he decided he'd phone his mother.

'Hello, Mumsie, it's me.'

'Darling, where *are* you? Are you all right? We thought you were coming home: Roger's mother told us –'

'I'm fine, Mumsie, and I *am* coming home. I'm on my way but I'm worried about Father, how he'll be with me, you know, with the exams and everything?'

'I'll speak to him, darling, it'll be all right. Actually he's uncharacteristically approachable at the moment, having finally acquired that nightclub he used to get apoplectic about: Hackers. He's turned into a pussycat, as the Americans say.'

'I'm sorry, Mumsie, I doubt I'll ever manage to think of Father as a pussycat: Bengal tiger's as close as I'll get, but if you really think it'll be all right . . .'

'I *know* it will, darling. Oh, he might *bluster* a bit – you know what he's like – but it'll blow over. Come home, Mark, *please*.'

'All right, Mumsie, I'll be there some time tomorrow, but I'll leave again if anything happens and this time I *won*'t be back.'

'Nothing will happen, darling, you have my word. Listen: why don't I come for you now, in the car?'

'*No*. No, Mumsie, it's all right, I've a couple of things to see to first. I'll make my way. Bye.'

Forty-seven

'Dennis! Dennis *Clissold*.'

Shit! He recognized Teresa Summerscales's voice and put a spurt on. He'd left Tim and Michael in the park and was off home. He was happy for Tim, but he was skint and hadn't had a drink and the last thing he needed was a lecture from a nosy cow like Summerscales. He thought he'd lose her by dodging through the crowd, but he was wrong. A clawlike hand descended on his shoulder and he was forced to turn. 'Oh, *hi*, Mrs Summerscales.' His smile suggested she was some gorgeous chick he'd been fantasizing about for months.

'Are you flipping *deaf*, Dennis Clissold? I've been calling you.'

'*Have* you? Sorry, I was miles away. How's it going?'

'It's going all right with me, lad, it's *you* I'm concerned about.'

'Me? Why, what have *I* done?'

'Well for one thing, you've taken to hanging around those dirty, drunken creatures who loll about in Market Square, swearing and shouting. I've seen you with them twice lately. What can you be *thinking* of, Dennis, keeping company with people like them?'

Dennis shrugged. 'One of those *creatures* just saved my mate's life, Mrs Summerscales.'

'What're you *talking* about, saved your mate's life? Can't save *themselves*, fellas like that, let alone other folk. D'you think your mam's struggled to give you a decent home so's you can mix with rubbish like them?'

'She might have.' *None of your business, you sad crone.* 'Anyway I don't mix with 'em. I say hello now and then, that's all.'

'Aye, well.' The woman looked at him. 'I know you think I'm an interfering old so-and-so, Dennis, but me and your mam go back a long way. I was there for her when she was having all that bother with your dad and I'll tell you something, you're starting to remind me of him.'

'So?' He scowled. 'What's wrong with that, plenty of guys look like their dad.'

She shook her head. 'Not *looks*, Dennis, I'm not on about looks. It's the way fellas like him *move* somehow, the way they avoid meeting people's eyes as if . . . oh, I don't know, as if they're *ashamed* of themselves and defiant at the same time. They don't *walk* down the street, they sort of *swagger* as if to say, yes, we both know what

I am and I *dare* you to give me a dirty look. And at the same time they're sort of *slinking*, like something nocturnal that's been caught out in daylight.' She shook her head. 'I can't describe what I mean, but your father moved like that and I can see it in you. Pretending you hadn't heard me's part of it.'

'I *didn*'t hear you.'

'No, your dad developed that, Dennis. It's called selective deafness. The patient hears what he wants to hear and nothing else. Selective blindness often develops at the same time. Listen.' She grabbed his shirtsleeve, forcing him to stop. 'There's an old song, "You Are My Sunshine". D'you know it?'

Passers-by were looking. Dennis sighed, nodded. 'Heard it, I think.'

'Well, you're your *mam's* sunshine, Dennis. There hasn't been much sunshine in her life – it's been clouds mostly – but when you get that place at university the sun'll show through and your mam'll get the bit of brightness she deserves.' She gazed into his eyes. 'Think about it, lad: don't take her sunshine away.'

Forty-eight

Mark had nothing to see to first, but he'd paid for his room and besides it'd be too quick, whisked home to Garton Hall before he'd time to get his head right. *One more quiet night.*

He didn't sleep well. His imagination had shot a selection of videos under the heading HOW IT MIGHT GO, and they played back all night inside his skull. They all started the same: he was walking up the marble steps to the front door of the Hall, feeling nervous. His mother didn't appear but her voice was there, urging him on. *'Go on, darling, there's nothing to be afraid of.'* It was as he crossed the threshold that the videos began to differ from one another, though they all featured Sir Ralph. *Best supporting actor.* In the nicest one the great man stumbled towards his son, with open arms and tears of joy on his cheeks, going, *'Mark, my dear, dear son, how I have wronged you.'* Yeah, right.

In each of the others the situation got gradually worse, and the last was pure horror. In this one, he'd barely stepped on to the chequered tiles when his father came roaring down the broad staircase brandishing one of those spiked clubs they fought with in medieval times. The roar echoed weirdly in the spacious hallway. As Mark turned to flee, his mother slammed the door in his face. A split-second later the club smashed into the back of Mark's neck, driving his face into the solid oak. As he collapsed, his face slid down the door, leaving a trail of slime like a slug, except that this slime had teeth in it.

It was another good breakfast. When the girl brought his coffee, Mark asked about buses. It looked like another hot day and he didn't feel up to a hike. She told him four buses ran to Lashford, the first at eight-fifteen.

If he hurried, he might just catch it: the next wasn't till ten-fifteen.

He'd no packing to do and he'd paid his bill. He left his breakfast unfinished but that was all right: he hadn't much of an appetite. The bus stop was across the green, near the seat he'd watched the ducks from. As he walked across the dewy grass his heart sank: the drunk was sitting on the seat.

Mark pretended he hadn't seen him. There were four women at the bus stop. He tagged on the end of the queue, hands in pockets, looking at the ground but it was no use. He heard shuffling footsteps, felt a tap on his shoulder. 'Morning, Charles. Off to Midborough, are we?'

'*I* am.' The four women were giving him dirty looks. *Good grief, they think I know the guy.*

'I've to get to Midborough myself,' Jim smarmed, 'chance of a job. One snag: no dosh.'

'Empty the poor box again, did they?' If Mark hoped to get rid of the man by being rude to him, he was doomed to disappointment. Jim was immune to embarrassment. 'Yes they did,' he growled, '*and* they never replaced the wine, *and* nobody fed the ducks. I'm not coming *here* again.'

The bus appeared, orbiting the green. The drunk clutched Mark's sleeve. 'Stand us the ride, lad, *please*: it's a hell of a walk in this boiling heat and I'm not young like you.' The bus hissed to a halt, stood shuddering. The women got on. Mark tried to shake off the drunk's grip but Jim had been shaken before. As the boy moved forward he kept pace, going sideways like a crab, his eyes pleading. Mark was afraid the driver would go without him. 'All right,' he snapped, 'only let go my sleeve and *don't* sit with me.'

'Oh *thanks*, Charles,' babbled the drunk, 'you don't know what it means.'

Mark knew what it meant. It meant he'd been a plonker. Furious with himself for having caved in, he stomped upstairs, hearing Jim follow. He went right to the front, flung himself into a seat and stared out of the window, deducting two pounds twenty from forty-seven pounds ninety-five in his head. *Forty-five seventy-five*. He felt the drunk slam down behind him, smelt pollcat. The bus rolled forward. Spaxton Market was left behind.

Forty-nine

'Dennis!'

He groaned, turned over, tugged the duvet over his head. His mother's call had penetrated a dream in which he'd been sitting on a lavatory in the middle of an open field, trying desperately to wipe his bum, pull up his trousers and slip away before Teresa Summerscales and Rodgers from Wicklow's, approaching hand in hand singing 'You Are My Sunshine', noticed him. His relief at having escaped this embarrassing predicament was spoiled by his awareness that today was Thursday, the day the exam results would be posted on the bulletin board at Thomas Cranmer Comp.

'Dennis, it's eight o'clock, time you were up.'

'Yeah, all right.' He kicked back the duvet, squinted at the bar of sunlight where the curtains didn't quite meet, swung his legs to the floor. *Why the rush, Mam: you've already* got *the only sunshine you'll see today*. Dread like lead in the pit of his stomach. *The lead of dread*. He stood up and reached for his jeans.

He didn't enjoy breakfast. Mam acted bright, but the hope in her eyes was desperate. She manipulated kettle, toaster and chitchat, avoiding both the subject and Dennis's eyes. Jimmy and Marie were unusually subdued as well. A household in denial.

He got out at eight forty-five; couldn't stand it any more. In the doorway he said, 'I'll see you later then, Mam.'

Susan, at the sink, turned her head. 'Come straight back, d'you hear, with your news.'

'Course. See you, Jimmy, Marie.' *Nothing'll be the same though*. He closed the door.

Michael was leaning on a lamp post at the end of Peartree Gardens. There was no sign of Tim yet. Michael grinned. 'Moment of truth, my man.'

Dennis sighed, pulled a face. 'Yeah. I don't half wish I'd done it different . . . my poor mam.'

Michael nodded. 'Know what you mean. Still, no use worrying about that now.' He looked at his watch. 'It's on the board, done with.'

Dennis chuckled, remembering his dream.

Michael looked at him. 'What?'

'I had this weird dream. Lavatory in the middle of a field. No building, just this bog with me on it, and my boss and a friend of my Mam's coming towards me. I'm like, "*Oh no, they'll spot me any second: where's the cowing paper?*"'

'What happened?'

'Dunno: Mam woke me up.'

'Shame.' Michael grinned. 'Means you're insecure, you know, dream like that. I read about it.'

'I don't need a dream to tell me. Mam says she'll chuck me out, I don't get the passes.'

'Oh yeah but she *won't*, my man. Parents say stuff like that, they don't mean it. They hope it'll make you try harder.'

'Not Mam. She didn't say it till *after*.'

'Oh well, you can always join the Circle.'

'Thanks a *bunch*, mate.' He shivered, though the sun was hot.

'Morning, chaps.' Tim sounded like Brasso as Major Henshaw. 'Here it is, the dawn of our golden age. Couple of years from now we'll all be up at Cambridge, punting the Backs.'

'Shut your gob, Timmo,' growled Dennis, 'just 'cause you're off the hook with Donny Conway.'

Tim looked pained, stayed in character. 'I say, old man, promise me you'll *buck up*. 'Tisn't the end of the world, y'know.'

They set off down Orchard Way, their long morning shadows in front of them.

Fifty

'Live in Midborough, do you?' asked the drunk, leaning forward in his seat.

Mark shook his head.

'Know people there then?'

'No.'

'Oh. So where will you stay?'

'Don't know yet.' He wasn't about to give this pest his parents' address. 'What about you?'

'Me?' Jim chuckled. 'Don't worry about me, I'll be all right.'

'I'm *not* worried: you've a job lined up, haven't you?'

'Huh? Oh yeah, the job. First week's wage, find a little room somewhere, try not to get kicked out like last time.'

'Good.' Mark sat forward a bit, hoping Jim would take the hint and shut up. Instead he leaned even further, touched him on the shoulder. 'Here, know what I did?'

Mark sighed. 'When?'

'When he kicked me out.'

'Of course I don't know, how could I?'

'What I did was –' He glanced all around, lowered his voice – 'I bombed the place.'

'*Bombed?*' Mark was interested in spite of himself.

'Yeah, with petrol. What you do is, you get a bottle – milk bottle or something – and you fill it with –'

'Yes, I know about petrol bombs, we did 'em in history at school. You mean you wrecked your room with one?'

'Not just the room, lad. You can't just bomb one room. The whole bleeding place went up.'

Mark turned, gazed at the drunk. 'That's . . . that's awful. I mean, weren't there *people* in the building?'

Jim shook his head. 'Not when I done it, no. I'm no murderer. I waited till all the fellas was out, then let 'er rip.' He laughed out loud. 'Serves the tight bogger right: four guys he had in there, all paying rent, and houses all over town. Rolling in it he was, and he kicks me out for the sake of a few measly quid. Bet he wishes he hadn't though.'

'But . . .' Mark frowned. 'Didn't he *know* it was you? You had a grudge. I'd have thought the police would've come for you straight away.'

Jim winked. 'Have to *find* me first, don't they, and Spaxton Market's not the sort of place they'd look for someone like me. You've got to be sharp, see: one step ahead all the time.'

The bus stopped. Mark looked out and saw the Chequered Skipper. Lithgow then. Some passengers came upstairs, and this seemed to faze Jim because, to Mark's relief, he leaned back in his seat and closed his eyes.

As the bus approached Lashford, the drunk seemed to be sleeping. Mark hoped he'd stay asleep and miss his stop, but there was no such luck. As the vehicle slowed and Mark got up, Jim roused himself and followed the lad out on to the pavement. Irritated, Mark turned on him. 'Look: I'm fed up of you following me all the time. We don't know each other, I've done what you asked, now leave me alone or I'll tell the first policeman I see about that petrol bomb.'

'Petrol bomb?' The drunk frowned, then grinned. 'Oh, the *petrol bomb*.' He laughed. 'You don't want to go believing everything people tell you, lad. There was no petrol bomb: that was just one of the little stories I tell to pass the time. Anyway you *haven't*: not yet.'

'Haven't *what*?'

'Done what I asked. Stand me the ride, I said. I meant to Midborough, this is Lashford. How'm I supposed to get to Midborough from here? What about my job?'

'Job?' Mark sneered. 'Know what *I* think? I think this job's about as real as your petrol bomb. Anyway *I* didn't mean Midborough: I doubt I've enough money for two tickets to Midborough.'

'How much you got?'

'None of your damn business.'

'If you've got forty, it's enough.'

'If I spent forty I'd be left with about eight pounds.'

'And if you didn't I'd be left with a sixty-mile hike and nothing at the end of it.' Jim smiled sadly. 'Could you do that to your fellow man, Charles? *Could* you?'

They walked side by side to the station. Mark bought two standard-class tickets. They went through to the platform. The train wasn't due for fifty-five minutes. It was very hot. Every bench was occupied, but there was a table in the cafeteria. It looked nice and cool in there. Jim looked at Mark. 'I don't know about you, Charles, but my throat's as dry as dust. They've got beer in there,

nice cold beer, and if I had money – eight pounds, say –
I know what *I'd* be doing for the next fifty-five
minutes, and it wouldn't be standing out here getting
sunstroke.'

Mark could see Jim's point. He was thirsty himself.
He was scared too: scared to be going home. A beer
might make him a bit less scared, and it would certainly
take care of his thirst. They went inside. Mark got two
beers. After a bit he got two more. Jim thought about
fools and Mark thought about petrol bombs.

Fifty-one

Oh no: hell's teeth, no. Dennis, in the middle of a scrum
of jostling kids, stared at the board. He'd known it was
going to be bad, but not *this* bad. *English . . . I'm* ace *at
English: got a B in the mocks. How the* heck's *it come out E?
And RE.* Everybody *passes RE.* Braced against the crush,
he read it again from the top and it came out the same –
eight subjects: one E, the rest Fs. He gave up, let himself
be shoved sideways and back, tears blurring his vision. A
knot of cheering girls reeled by, clutching one another.
They spun him round and passed on oblivious, like a
supertanker running down a smack.

'That bad, huh?' Tim. Embarrassed by his tears,
Dennis swiped the back of a hand across his eyes and
nodded. 'Bad as it gets.'

'Straight Fs?'

'Just about. E in English.'

'Same as me. Scraped Cs in Maths and French though, Christ knows how.'

'You done good.' More envious than pleased.

'My folks won't think so.'

Michael joined them. 'So how'd it go, men?'

They told him and he shrugged. 'Blessed is he who expects nothing, for he shall not be disappointed. Straight Fs, me.'

They drifted between knots of their year group, some jubilant, others subdued. It was only twenty past nine. The day stretched ahead, bright but not with promise. They weren't in a rush to get home.

'Park?' suggested Tim, and the others nodded, not because they felt like communing with nature but because, the way they were feeling, it didn't much matter where they went.

It was quiet in the park. Sunlight slanting through a thin mist hit the dewy grass and shattered into a billion rainbow sparkles that scintillated unnoticed by the glum trio. They made their way to the old gazebo and sat in the gloom without speaking, staring at the floor. If at that moment a fairy godmother had materialized with the power to turn back the clock a few weeks, the three would have vowed to do it all differently this time. They'd have meant it too, but they'd all have broken their vow because, bit by bit, without noticing, they'd fallen under the spell of a mighty genie: The Genie of the Can, whose magic is so powerful no outside agency can prevail against it.

Not even a fairy godmother.

Fifty-two

'Dennis . . . oh, our Dennis.' Susan Clissold held on to the kitchen table with both hands. Its corner thrust into her skirt at thigh level. Her head was bowed, her mouth open. A dewdrop quivered on the tip of her nose. Distress too deep for decorum.

Dennis, by the fridge, wished himself anywhere but here, anytime but now. Again, he'd known it would be bad but found himself once more appalled at *how* bad. His mother's state of stunned incapacity brought back the scene in *Dolores Clayborn* where Dolores's husband fetches her a mighty thwack over the kidneys with a lump of wood. She doesn't scream, doesn't make a sound: the pain's too great for that. She stands propped, much as his mother is standing now, waiting for it to ebb a little so she can start to regain control of her body. His response to that fictitious incident remains vivid: upsurge of pity for the hardworking, unappreciated woman, utter contempt for the cowardly, useless man. *He's me, that guy, except I'm worse: at least he didn't do it to his* mother.

'Mam . . .'

'*Don't*, our Dennis. Don't you touch me, don't come *near*.' She lifted her head, pushed her hair back with her hand, fished in her pocket for a tissue, mopped and blew. 'Your dad was a dab hand at that: breaking my

116

heart, then fawning round me as if his arm round my waist and a few soft words'd make everything all right.' She turned to face him. 'Aye, *he* could turn on the waterworks when it suited him so you're wasting your time: I'm immune. You'd better get up to your room or somewhere, our Dennis. *Anywhere* out of my sight. Kids'll be home anytime.'

Well. He slumped on his bed, gazing at his wan features in the dressing-table mirror. *You* wanted *this, didn't you, you donkey? No more school, stay on at Wicklow's, hang out with your mates, dosh for tinnies, dosh for Hackers. Now you've* got *it, so what're you bawling about?*

It was a reasonable point, but it seemed to cut no ice with his reflection.

Fifty-three

''Scuse me, Mr Rodgers?'

'Blimey!' The supervisor glanced at his clock. 'Miracles will never cease: Dennis Clissold, *early.*'

'I came early to ask you something.'

'Oh aye?' He studied the boy's face. 'You been crying, lad?'

'No, I got something in my eye, that's all.'

'Ah-ha.' Rodgers sat back, folded his arms. 'Go on then.'

'Thing is, Mr Rodgers, I could do with more hours.'

'Huh! It's only the other day I had you in here 'cause you weren't managing the hours you've got already.'

'I know, and I've been trying to do better.'

The man nodded. 'I noticed, Dennis, but I don't know that Viv and Ernest'd be all that thrilled and, besides, it makes a lot of work in the office, changing someone's hours. I'm not sure it's worth it, just for three or four weeks.'

Dennis frowned. 'Three or four weeks?'

'Yes: that's when schools go back, isn't it?'

'Oh right, I see what you mean, Mr Rodgers, only you see, I won't be going back to school. I've left.'

'Ah.' Rodgers made the swivel chair arc left and right a few times, like the brass balls of a carriage-clock. 'Results day, of course. My lad got four As, how'd *you* do?'

Dennis flushed, stared at the concrete floor. 'Not great, Mr Rodgers.'

'No . . .?' The supervisor looked him in the eye. 'Leaving, lad: your mother's idea, or your own?'

None of your rotten business. 'Neither: they won't *let* me go on with my results.'

'There's re-sits, surely?'

'Well yeah, but like . . .'

'You *can't* just throw the towel in, Dennis, not when your future depends on it. What about your mother, she'll be a bit upset, won't she?'

A bit upset. 'Yeah, a bit. That's why I want the hours, Mr Rodgers – start bringing some dosh in.'

'Look, lad.' The supervisor unfolded his arms, rested his palms on his knees and sighed. 'I've been with

Wicklow's ten years. They're a decent firm. Far be it from me to run 'em down, but a lad like you, you're *wasted* here. Packing's all right as an evening job, or for the likes of Viv and Ernest who lost their real jobs through redundancy, or for people without qualifications.' He shook his head. 'I'm sorry, Dennis, I'm leaving your hours as they are, and when school starts again I want you to walk into this cubicle and tell me you're swotting for re-sits. All right?'

Fifty-four

Packing's not Viv's day job. She operates an ice-cream van in the daytime, moonlights at Wicklow's. Mr Rodgers doesn't know this.

Viv doesn't like holding down two jobs, but ice-cream's up and down. Spell of warm weather you can make three, four hundred a week easy. Get a wet patch, even in summer, and it'll go as low as sixty. She doesn't make a bomb at Wicklow's but it's steady, or could be if that smart-mouth kid'd keep his act together. Two youngsters and a husband on the scrapheap's kept her moonlighting for a year and a half now, but all that could change.

See, Viv and Ken (Ken is Viv's husband) have this friend. His name doesn't matter. What matters is, his job as a long-distance truckie takes him to the continent on a regular basis. France and Spain. Now the point of the continent is, you can get booze and ciggies there for a fraction of what you'd pay in England. You have it to carry, of course, but with a rig like this guy drives it isn't a problem. So, he stocks up every trip and it's a nice little sideline because you can charge twice what you paid and the stuff's still cheap enough to attract the punters.

One snag. Because he's got so much room in his rig, this friend of Viv and Ken's is bringing over more than he can flog. Much more. His garage looks like a bonded flipping warehouse. Well, he's away a lot, see? Can't get round the customers, and this is where Viv comes in. Viv and her ice-cream van.

It's dead easy once word gets around. There's never any shortage of punters, because the law makes it hard for some people to get their booze through shops and supermarkets. Young people. They can't get served in pubs either. They can sometimes get a drink at a club, but clubbing's expensive and they have to lie about their age, whereas anyone can use an ice-cream van.

Viv's been dealing the canned stuff for a while now. Building a clientele around the estates of Midborough. It's amazing how many people appear when she gives 'em a quick burst of 'Greensleeves' on the chime. Amazing how young some of them are too, and they don't all want a ninety-nine with raspberry sauce. She's so busy at some stops it's almost a traffic hazard, which is awkward. Well, you don't want to bother the police, they've enough to do as it is.

Trade's so good now, Viv finds herself having to break off and re-stock the van two or three times a day. Pity to have to bother with the ice-cream really: takes up a lot of room and the profit margin's poor, but it's a case of no ice-cream, no van, so there you go. And of course it's camouflage. Anyway, the other day her friend the truckie says, 'Viv, why don't you jack in the Wicklow's job, do an evening round?'

Well why not? Whole different clientele, evenings. Be good in winter too: nice and dark, and lager's not seasonal. Not like ice-cream.

She's giving it serious consideration.

Fifty-five

The warm spell broke in the early hours of Friday with a spectacular thunderstorm. The torrential rain drove Yomper from his skip. He wrapped a bin bag round his head and scuttled across town to where Digby, Cow and Brasso lay dry inside a rusting boiler on derelict land by the railway line.

Mark Penfold, newly arrived in town, spent a miserable night under the concrete entrance ramp of Midborough's multi-storey car park. The protection it afforded was minimal and there was only the ground to sit on, but he'd spent the last of Marigold's dosh on beer for Jim and himself and beggars can't be choosers. He'd ample time to recall wistfully his snug bed at Meldilorn, where sprigs of peppermint and rosemary sweetened the night.

Dennis had a warm bed but couldn't sleep. A silly

notion squatted like a toad on his mind: that he was the cause of the storm. His criminally irresponsible behaviour over the past months had called down these flashes, this lashing rain, the crashing peals of thunder. He'd aroused the wrath of something huge that was showing its displeasure. This whole thing was aimed at *him*.

Donny Conway was having a poor night, but not because of the storm. Donny cared no more about storms than he did about his immortal soul. What he *did* care about, what made him smoulderingly angry, was the thought of somebody pulling the wool over his eyes, making a monkey out of him.

The cause of Donny's insomnia was as follows. Crossing Market Square the previous afternoon, a minder – one of the three who'd breakfasted with him Wednesday – had glanced at a row of winos sitting on a wall and had seen a face he thought he recognized. He couldn't place it at first, then he remembered: the wino was a dead ringer for that scruffy vicar who'd come bothering the boss at the Italia the other morning. Now this minder was no professor – it was a tussle for him to walk and think at the same time without walking into something – and for a minute or two his mind humped itself sluggishly round thoughts of twin brothers, plastic surgery and sheer coincidence. By the time it occurred to him that the wino and the vicar were probably one and the same and he'd hurried back to the square, the quartet had moved on. All the minder could do was tell Donny what he'd seen.

Now, as the wind blew the storm away and Midborough dripped and glistened in fitful moonlight,

Brasso slept while Donny lay awake, plotting a revenge that might make the wino's slumbers permanent.

Fifty-six

Dennis dropped off as it started to get light and came awake to find Jimmy shaking him.

'Uh . . . *quit* it, you mollusc.'

'Mam says it's eight o'clock, she's off out and she wants a word with you before she goes.'

'Down in a minute, tell her.' What *word? Pack your kit . . . find a room . . . move in with your useless father . . .*

She looked washed-out, slumped at the kitchen table. The window behind her was grey, beaded with drizzle. *'Don't take her sunshine away.'* Well, he had. She didn't look at him as he spooned granules into a mug, gave the kettle a burst of power, poured. He came to the table, stirring; reached for the milk jug. 'Our Jimmy said –'

'Yes.' She sounded tired. 'Let's get one thing straight, Dennis, right now.' She stared into her mug. 'You're not leaving school.' He started to speak, she raised a hand to stop him. 'I *know* they won't have you in lower sixth, but you can swot like mad and re-sit your exams in November, and that's exactly what you're going to do. Either that, or you leave this house today and never come back.'

'Mam –?'

'*No.*' She clamped her palms to her ears, shook her

head. 'Don't say anything, unless it's "*Yes, Mam.*" Everything else – the "*sorrys*", the "*won't happen agains*", the "*wasn't my faults*" – I heard a hundred times from your father and it all meant nothing: absolutely nothing.'

'Yes, Mam.' He meant it, he really did. Teresa Summerscales was right. His mother had slaved year after year for a pittance down Yourprice, stacking shelves so *he'd* never have to; so that he might have the university education that would lift him and his children beyond the necessity of such employment for ever. *Yeah, and what've I done . . . chucked it away: chucked my mam's life away.*

No I haven't. There's November. I'll swot: I'll swot like no guy ever swotted. No more Michael, no more Tim. I'll tell 'em. I'll tell 'em this morning. No more lager either, no Red Bulls down Hackers. No Hackers. *From now on, work. Work, work, work. I* will *be your sunshine, Mam, you'll see.*

A van passed the house. An ice-cream van. On its floor, out of sight, stood a stack of cans, and in one can crouched a genie. As Dennis thought his highly commendable and totally sincere thoughts, the genie laughed. Like Susan Clissold, he'd heard it all before.

Fifty–seven

It was half past eight. The drizzle had died out but Mark's clothes were damp and he was chilled to the bone. He'd left the dubious shelter of the ramp at six, hoping to get warm by walking about. Not only had it not worked, it had sharpened his appetite: no good thing when you're flat broke. His first priority was to get some money, but *how*?

Leaning on a wall in the entrance recess of the market with his arms wrapped round himself, he constructed a fantasy in which he hitched out to Garton and loitered under the rhododendrons in the grounds of the Hall till his sister Jess came out. In his fantasy he called to her from the bushes and she ran to embrace him. They hugged on the lawn and Jess slipped him three hundred pounds.

He was jerked back to reality when a security man started unlocking the doors from inside. The market was open. The man had given him a dirty look through the glass, so he waited till he'd disappeared before going in to soak up some delicious warmth. Glancing around he noticed a jewellery stall with what looked like a lot of second-hand rings, which was handy because he was going to have to flog his watch. It was a good watch, a Longines: sixteenth birthday gift from his parents. It ought to raise enough for grub and a little bottle of something warming, as well as the big bottle of something even more warming he'd need later on.

First he needed a lavatory, and a bit of a wash wouldn't come amiss either. He located the toilets and did what he had to do, rounding off his ablutions with a long drink from the tap. He'd combed his hair and rubbed his teeth with a wet finger and was feeling a bit more human. With the watch in his pocket he made his way to the jewellery stall.

The stallholder was a stringy woman of about seventy with shrewd eyes, a purple shawl and too many rings on her veiny old hands. She sniffed as Mark deposited his watch on the counter. 'Not much call for those nowadays, boy. All digital, see.'

'It's a Longines, gold. These don't go out of style.' She wasn't going to best him like that oik of a landlord.

'Know it all, do you, boy?'

'I know it's a fine watch.'

'Mebbe you should hang on to it then, eh?'

'I would, but something's come up: bit of an emergency actually.'

'Aye.' She nodded, picking up the watch. Her rings flashed under the spotlights as she turned it this way and that. 'See a lot of emergencies, we do. Help where we can.' She peered at him over half-glasses. 'I can go to thirty.'

'You can go to . . .' He checked himself, extended his hand. 'Never mind, I'll try elsewhere.'

'Suit yourself, boy.' She laid the watch across his palm. 'Don't know of an *elsewhere* though, not in Midborough.'

'Then I'll *leave* Midborough.' He was desperate, starving, but he was damned if he'd let *her* see. He turned away.

'Just a minute, boy.' He turned. Her hand was out. 'I'll have another look.'

I bet *you will*. He handed it to her, feeling smug. She took off her specs, stuck a watchmaker's glass in her eye and made a big show of examining the watch. Mark's stomach rumbled. *Come* on, *you scrawny old grave-dodger: stop mucking about.*

She glanced up with the glass in place, looking remarkably like a chameleon. 'I might be able to move this. Fifty.'

'Seventy.'

'*Hoo* – fifty-five, final offer.'

'Sixty-five, least I'll take.'

'Take sixty, rob me blind.'

'Yes, OK.' The watch had cost four hundred. She'd come out best and she knew it; smiling, counting the notes on to his palm. 'There: emergency over.'

'Sure.' He walked away, stuffing the notes into his pocket. Earlier, huddled in the doorway he'd noticed a Thresher. He'd go there first, grab a spot of breakfast.

He left the market. Five men were sitting on a low wall. One was Jim. Their eyes met momentarily, but Jim's held no flicker of recognition. He'd no way of knowing the lad had money in his pocket again and a friend without dosh is as useful as a tin towel.

Fifty-eight

'Dennis, my man.' Michael's heartiness sounded forced, even over the phone. 'Where are you, why aren't you here?'

'I'm at home. I'm thinking of not coming today.'

'Whaddya mean, not *coming*? I'm not here just to

prop the post office up, you bivalve. Tim hasn't come either.'

'Are you surprised, mate? How did *your* folks take the wondrous news?'

Michael snorted. 'Put it this way: I'm not their all-time fave human being this morning. Breakfast was scary.'

'Same here. I'm under orders to re-sit in November: Tim's probably grounded.'

'*Why?* He passed Maths and French, for God's sake: the Einstein of Cranmer Comp, they're calling him.'

'Who's *they*, Michael? He got two Cs. Oxbridge won't fight over him.'

'OK, so we turn out not to be conspicuously academic: so *what*? It's still a beautiful world, my man. The sky's blue, tweetie-birds're singing, cans piled high in Thresher's window. Everything's just like before. All you've got to do is step out and get your share of it.'

'I *can't* mate, sorry. My mam's face. I'm swotting.'

'I'm swotting *too,* Den: I'm just not starting today, that's all. I'm in shock. So're you. So's Tim. Stands to reason, blow like that. We need the weekend to get over it: learn to laugh again. Monday we get stuck in. Make sense to you?'

'I suppose in a way, but . . .'

'Are you landed with the kids or something?'

'No, they've gone to their auntie's.'

'Well then, there's nothing to stop you. Get off the phone, get a life. I'll see you in a bit.'

'Hey just a *minute,* Mike: I haven't said I'll . . . hello?'

The gastropod's hung up. Dennis scowled at the mobile phone in his palm as though the instrument was somehow to blame. *Call him back, say no.* Why *though, when he's right? I am in shock. I need to talk to someone — someone in the same boat — then on Monday I'll be able to put it all behind me, make a fresh start.*

He put on his jacket, stuffed the phone in one pocket and his latchkey in another, then remembered he was broke. *Can't show up skint, can I?* He went through to the kitchen, carried a chair to the high cupboard and reached down the tin his mother put the occasional pound coin in. *My tights and stockings fund,* she called it. It tended to mount slowly, but she hadn't treated herself lately and the tin felt promisingly heavy.

There were fourteen pounds. Dennis thought he'd borrow five, then remembered Wicklow's would pay him tonight and upped it to seven. He'd put it back when she'd gone to bed so she'd never know; in which case he might as well . . .

He put the empty tin back on the shelf. It was the first tin he'd emptied today, but it wouldn't be the last.

Fifty-nine

It wasn't Glayva but it wasn't bad. Not wanting to down it in full view of passers-by, Mark had found an alley with a burnt-out shop and a skip. He'd nipped behind the skip. The small flat bottle was empty now, its former contents a comforting glow in his middle. He tossed it into Yomper's bedroom and walked out on to the street. *Might treat myself to another of those.*

Not yet though. Things to do. Three things. One: bite to eat. Two: Sir Ralph's latest toy. Three: room for tonight, no more sleepouts.

It surprised him how naked he felt without a watch. Wearing the Longines, he'd never consciously consulted it. Now he'd look at his wrist every few minutes, find nothing there and feel like a recent amputee. For the first time since early childhood he noticed public clocks. The one he was about to walk under was mounted over a jeweller's shop. It was twenty past nine.

He found a Starbucks, bought coffee and a Danish pastry, bagged a table. There were a few customers. Each time a table was vacated, a round blonde girl of about sixteen would appear with a dishcloth to wipe and tidy and square away the chairs. When she passed close to Mark's table he said, 'Excuse me?'

'Get you something, sir?'

He shook his head. 'D'you know Hackers, the club?'

'Course.'

'How would I find it from here?'

'Hmmm . . .' She thought for a moment. 'D'you know Market Square?'

'Yes.'

'Well when you get to Market Square, look for Infirmary Road. You can't miss it: it's dead opposite

Thresher.' She looked at him. 'On foot, are you?'

'Yes.'

Well, walk along Infirmary Road till you see Bridge Street on the right. Hackers is about fifty metres along on the left, set back a bit. Not open now though.'

'No, I know.' He smiled. 'Thanks.'

'Welcome.' She took his empty plate, hurried away.

He finished his coffee and left. His clothes had dried out. He felt cool, *focused*: first time in months.

The girl's directions had been spot-on. He stood in Bridge Street, studied the building opposite. Sir Ralph's new toy. Nothing special from the outside. Old warehouse by the look of it. Blackened brick, four storeys. Incongruous glass porch stuck on the front, modest sign over the door in cursive script: Hackers. Locked up tight as a tick. Nobody about.

He crossed over. On one side, the club was joined on to the building next door, which looked empty. On the other, a narrow alleyway separated it from another former warehouse, now shared by several small businesses whose signs were screwed to the door. Four cars were parked at the kerb. Not wanting to be seen loitering, Mark slipped into the alleyway.

It was one and a half metres wide, dark, smelled of pee. He was treading on debris he couldn't see. Black walls both sides, the occasional small window high up, caked with grime. He pressed on to the end and emerged in a yard of greasy, littered cobbles. On his left, a ten-foot breeze-block wall topped off with razor-wire on Y-brackets showed how much the proprietors of the small businesses enjoyed having a club next door. To his right was a raised loading-bay with a massive sliding door that had a small door cut into it. Both doors were heavily padlocked. The yard ended at a high brick wall with a pair of dilapidated wooden gates, bolted and barred. Beyond the bay the building sported four fair-sized windows, one above the other.

Mark glanced about him. As far as he could see there was no CCTV. *Soon would be, Father in charge. Would have been, I mean.* Sir Ralph, having once been poor, was a believer in security.

Satisfied, he braved the alleyway again and headed back to the Square, where he'd noticed a tourist information centre. *Two down, one to go.*

Sixty

'Better late than never.'

'Shut it, you maggot. I shouldn't be here at all.'

'Fiddlesticks, my man. Observe.' Michael produced a billfold which he flipped open, revealing the edges of several banknotes. 'A modest advance, courtesy of my wrinklies.'

Dennis pulled a face. 'Nice of 'em, considering.'

'Oh, they don't *know*. I plundered Daddy's stash.'

'Yeah, well remember what nearly happened to Tim, doing that.'

'Chill *out*, man. I'll cover it, and *without* Donny

Conway's help. Come.' He pocketed the billfold. 'Let us seek the Circle.'

The alcoholics were on their bit of wall. Brasso squinted up at the boys. 'Where's your mate?'

Michael shrugged. 'Not playing out today: been a naughty boy.'

'*Again*?'

'Well yeah but not dosh this time: grades. Bad grades. Me and Dennis too.'

'*That* all?' Brasso's laugh rattled in his throat. 'Tell him not to worry: I never passed an exam in my life, didn't stop *me* gettin' where I am.'

Dennis thought Michael's laugh was strained as he fished out the billfold, handed Brasso a twenty. 'Brace of six-packs please, my man.'

Brasso accepted the note, stood up. 'Er . . . brace. That's two, right?'

The boy nodded. 'Was, when I was at school.'

'Oh yeah?' Cow grinned. 'And when *was* that exac'ly, young man?'

Michael ignored this, looked at Yomper. 'Is there a problem?'

'Not a *problem* exactly, more an embarrassment. See, there's five of us now, and one six-pack's stretching it a bit thin . . .'

'*Five*?' Michael frowned past the wino's shoulder at the wall. 'There's *four* of you, same as always. Just 'cause I flunked my exams doesn't mean I can't flipping *count*, you know.'

Brasso shook his head. 'It's five. New lad's popped into the market, brown-out. Back in a minute.'

133

'Ah.'

'And I thought, you know, being as I did your mate a favour the other day, you might . . .?'

'Sure.' Michael nodded. 'Make it three: four if you like.'

Brasso went off. Dennis watched him cross the square. A part of him was wishing he hadn't come; the rest yearned for that first, healing can. He watched till Brasso disappeared into Thresher, relieved that the poor sod hadn't spotted somebody who might be his mother. When he looked round, the Circle's new member was sitting on the wall.

It was his father.

Sixty-one

'*Dad?*' Dennis stared at the man next to Cow. Michael stared at *him*. 'He's your . . .?'

'Hello, son, how's it hanging?' Jim Clissold had lost some front teeth since he'd popped in to see his kids . . . what . . . two years ago? Three? He'd thinned too; hollow cheeks frosted with stubble, bony wrists emerging from the ragged cuffs of an old suit jacket. His tangled hair was completely white. Only the eyes; blue eyes so clear you could see the amused defiance lurking in their depths, had stayed the same.

'I'm . . . good, Dad. What're you doing . . . I mean *here*, with . . .?'

'With a bunch of drunks? I might ask *you* the same thing, our Den.' Jim shook his head, chuckling. 'Bet your mam doesn't know.' He looked up. 'How *is* she, son, your mam?'

'She's all right. Well . . . she's upset at the moment 'cause I made a mess of GCSE.'

'GCSE?' His father looked startled. 'You *that* age already? I thought . . .'

'I'm sixteen. Jimmy's twelve and our Marie's nine.'

'Good God!' He shook his narrow head. 'Little Marie, nine. Don't time fly when you're having fun?'

'*Are* you, Dad?'

'Huh: am I *what*?'

'Having fun?' It wasn't till his voice cracked he realized he was crying. He was dimly aware of Michael watching him, and his father's new mates.

'Hey!' Jim Clissold didn't get up but he spread his arms, palms outwards and looked concerned. 'Not *crying*, our Den: not for *me*.' On the word *me* the arms curled inwards till the fingertips touched the chest. 'You *knew*, surely: knew your old dad was an alkie. Your mam *must've* told you: she told *me* often enough.'

'She's told me, and I'm *not* crying.' Dennis swiped the back of a hand across his eyes. 'It's just . . . I *knew* you liked a few pints and that, but like, I thought you *worked*. You did, last time we saw you. You told us. Job in a computer factory. I've pictured you there ever since.'

'Ah well.' His father shook his head. 'You don't want to go *picturing*, son. Worst thing you can do. I used to picture your mam, after she blew me out. You kids as well, but mostly your mam. I'd catch myself wondering what she was doing, *right now, this minute*; and I'd picture her doing it.' He shook his head again. 'Gave me pain, that did. Lot of pain, so in the end I jacked it in. Upped my prescription instead: the lotion as before, only more. That's how come I lost the job.'

'And the room. You had a room over a hairdresser's?'

'Phew! What a *memory*! Don't know how you could've fouled up those exams, memory like you've got.' He nodded. 'Lost that as well, got behind with the rent.'

'So where . . .?'

'Do I doss down now? Doorways, son, same as these guys. Railway arches. Anywhere we can find.'

Dennis gazed at his father, shook his head. 'I don't know if I can stand to *think* about my dad in some doorway, wet night, windy. It wasn't too bad, thinking about that room over the hairdresser, even though I didn't know where it was. You were dry and warm, in a bed somewhere. *Now* . . .'

'Here we go then!' Yomper jostled Dennis, bent to deposit six-packs on the wall. Digby tore into a pack, passed up cans, started on another. Jim Clissold passed a can to Dennis, ripped the tab from his own and raised it in a toast. 'The lotion: to be taken before, with or instead of food. Cures picturing, promotes forgetting. Cheers.'

Sixty-two

Mark entered the tourist information centre, approached the counter. The woman behind it smiled. 'Good morning, how may I help you?'

'I'm looking for a room. Single, two nights, central. Around twenty pounds a night.'

'Twenty?' The assistant arched her brow. 'I don't know if we've got . . . just a minute.' She tapped a keyboard, peered at a screen. 'There's one. The Railway Hotel. Eighteen-fifty a night.' She looked apologetic. 'It's not a very nice area.'

He told her that didn't matter and, no, she needn't call them. If she'd please direct him he'd walk over there now, register. She unfolded a town map, turned it so he could see, traced a route with a scarlet fingernail. He thanked her and left.

She watched him go, a small frown between her eyes. Funny lad. Crumpled somehow, and apparently no luggage. Any other guesthouse she'd have called to warn them, but The Railway . . . She shrugged, refolded the map, thought about something else.

It wasn't a very nice area, and the proprietor matched his surroundings. 'That's thirty-seven, in advance, breakfast not included. Round key opens the front door, flat key's for the room. No drink, no music, no women, and if you come in after eleven do it quietly. Vacate by ten Sunday morning, leave the towel.'

His room was on the second floor back, the view an expanse of litter-strewn waste ground with mounds of broken brick and rank weeds. A cylindrical boiler lay rusting in the middle distance. He'd nothing to unpack and nowhere to go so after counting his money, down to sixteen fifty-five, he shed his trainers and stretched out on the bed, which sagged in the middle like his bed at school. Within ten seconds of closing his eyes he was asleep.

Sixty-three

'So listen, son, *listen*.' Jim Clissold draped an arm round his son's shoulders. 'Your old man's been around, right?'

Dennis wasn't paying attention. He'd drunk two, three cans, maybe six, and was trying to listen to Brasso on his other side, telling Michael about a loan he'd extracted from a widow in Morecambe some years back when he was being Major Henshaw. He could tell it was a good tale by the way Michael was laughing, but his father kept pulling him away and in the end he couldn't be bothered to go on resisting. He relaxed, sighed. 'Right.'

'Right, so he should know what he's talking about?'
'Yes.'

'OK, so here's a bit of whatsit . . . advice. First off,

don't worry about your mam. Don't *ever* worry about her, she's tough. Tougher than . . than you think.' He chuckled, shaking his head. '*I* worried about her, son. *Years* I worried about your mam: what she'd do if I . . . you know, did my own thing. How she'd manage and that. Well, she managed all right, didn't she? *You'd* know, you were there. Didn't she do well?'

Dennis shrugged under his father's arm. 'I suppose.' *She* didn't *though, did she? Not really*. Anyway he wasn't going to think about his mother. Not today, not tomorrow either. Michael had suggested Hackers tomorrow night: one last rave before the swotting took over. He shook his head. 'I'm not worried, Dad.'

'Tha's the whatsit, son . . . spirit. Next off, don't get het up about *exams* and all like that, 'cause what *exams* are, see −' he swigged from his can, wiped his lips with the back of his hand − 'what *exams* are, is a con trick to get you in the rat race. See, *I* did all that. Homework, field trips, revising, exams, and for *what*? I'll tell you for what, shall I?' He scowled at his son, who nodded. 'So I could work my tabs off for the rest of my life, making some other bogger rich. Well *no*. Thank you very much, but not *me*.' Taking his arm from Dennis's shoulder he hurled the empty can into some shrubs. 'Not Jimmy Clissold: you don't get *me* like that.'

As his father fumbled a fresh can from the pack beside him, Dennis stood up. Even in his fuddled state, a part of him recognized the ludicrousness of taking the advice of a man so useless his wife had kicked him out of the family home; a man incapable of keeping either a job or a roof over his head; a man who no longer knew the ages of his children; a man with absolutely nothing to show for forty years of living except a wreck of a body in a ragbag of other people's cast-off clothes. Dennis stood up because he suspected his father was about to mention freedom; the importance of being free. He didn't think he could stand that.

'Wh . . . where you *off*, our Den?' Jim looked up, struggling to focus his eyes. 'Something to say to you, son. Important.'

'Sorry, Dad.' Dennis shook his head. 'I've gotta split. Work tonight.' He produced a grin. ''Sbeen nice though, seeing you again. I'll tell Mam you're OK, right?'

'There y'*go*, see, rushing off like a bull at a gate, can't wait to make some other bogger rich. Go on then.' Waving his son away with both arms. 'Sod off, waste of time talking to you. And listen.'

'What?'

'You tell your mam *nothing*, right? Nothing about me, 'cause she don't want to know. Cow gave a toss about me, wouldn't have blown me out in the first place. Understand?'

'Sure, Dad.' He looked at Michael. 'You coming?'

Michael nodded, got up. 'We'll see you guys tomorrow, right?'

Nods and grunts from the drunks. As the boys crossed the square Michael said, 'Hey, Den, that guy *really* your old man?'

'No.' Dennis kicked a styrofoam carton across the flags. 'He's a guy who sometimes *disguises* himself as my old man so I'll buy him booze.'

Michael didn't believe this, but something in his friend's voice warned him not to pursue the matter. They walked on in silence, Dennis wishing what he'd said was true.

Sixty-four

They've gone and told the new guy all about it. His mother, the Yourprice bag, everything. Always good for a laugh, see. He laughed all right, that Jim. Damn near fell off the wall.

It's late now: time to leave Market Square before some nine-year-old copper shows up looking for a cushy arrest. Drunk and incapable. Trouble is, the new guy'll tag along with Cow and Digby, doss down in the boiler, and Brasso doesn't feel like being matey with somebody he doesn't know from Adam, but who knows all about him. When the others get up and move off he hangs back, pretending to suck the last drop from a can that ran dry an hour ago.

There's a spot at the back of the bakery on Garton Road where warm air comes through a grating in the wall. He's never used it in summer, but there's nothing to stop him kipping there tonight and who knows, maybe that Jim'll move on tomorrow.

He shuffles through the town centre and sets off along Garton Road. It's a long one. Further out where the bakery is it gets quite rural, but first there's a run-down district of crumbling terraces, vandalized kiosks and doomed corner shops. There isn't much traffic at this time of night and Brasso seems to have the road to himself. If he turned suddenly and looked behind he'd see he was being followed, but any sixth sense Brasso might once have possessed succumbed long ago to alcohol and was drowned.

Where shops and houses start to thin, there's a derelict filling-station that used to advertise itself as the last in town. There are no pumps on its dusty forecourt now, just litter, but the pay-station cum shop still stands, brick walls graffitied, windows boarded up. Brasso turns in, slants across the forecourt and nips behind the building for a pee.

He's zipping up when he hears boots on cement and a voice purrs, 'Evening, reverend.' A half-turn's all he's managed when the baseball bat comes down. There's a sound like an apple splitting and Brasso crumples to the ground. Two big men look down at him. One slides a toecap under the body, lifts it a little, lets it flop back. When his companion shoots him an inquiring glance he shakes his head and says, 'He's there, mate.' He means heaven.

On a bench two hundred miles away a bag-lady grunts, lifts her head, peers blearily across the midnight park. Something has woken her but it's gone now, whatever it was. Her head sinks. Her chin touches her chest. She sleeps. For the first time in many years, nobody is seeking her.

Sixty-five

Two things happened in the packing department at Wicklow's that night. Everybody got paid, and Viv gave a week's notice. When Rodgers asked why she was leaving, Viv said she was fed-up having her earning power sabotaged by people who can't be bothered turning up on time. She mentioned no names, and the word booze didn't come up either.

Dennis had spent his mother's tights and stockings fund lubricating his father but that was all right: he could easily replace the fourteen pounds now. Well, not *easily*. He'd drawn forty-four pounds sixty, which was a bit less than average because he'd been late a time or two. Forty-four sixty less fourteen leaves thirty sixty. The new boss of Hackers had jacked up admission to eight quid, which left twenty-two sixty. You could bet your boots drinks'd be up as well. A Red Bull used to set you back two-fifty under the previous boss; it'd be two seventy-five now, maybe three quid. Twenty-two sixty wasn't going to go far at that rate, especially when you've to keep some back for a taxi home.

Still, it's a final fling, isn't it? Last time ever, so why don't I hang on to the fourteen, pay it back next week when all I'll be doing is swotting? Mam never gets the tin down. Well, hardly ever. It'll just be bad luck if she decides to get it down in the next few days. And it's dead money, stuck on top of that

143

cupboard. Dead money. Might as well be doing something. No point having dosh and not enjoying it.

Makes sense, right?

Sixty-six

Saturday, two-twenty a.m. Police Constable Stables on foot patrol in Garton Road. Waste of time in his view: nothing here worth pinching. He's seen an old van rattling towards town and a black cat sniffing a lamp post. Now, to complete his enjoyment it's starting to drizzle. He'll keep on as far as the old filling-station, walk back on the other side. If it comes on heavier he'll stand in a doorway and have a crafty drag.

He nearly doesn't bother with the filling-station. What's the point, it's empty. Now and then some dosser'll kick out a board and squeeze inside for a kip, but so what? Worst that could happen is he'd set the place on fire, and that'd be no loss. No petrol there now. He's tempted to cross the road and start back but he's a conscientious officer, and what's a few more yards?

Under the awning he stands on dry cement. Maybe if he waits a bit the drizzle will ease. He looks towards the pay-station. All the boards are intact, this side anyway. There's something on the ground, there on the corner. Small heap. Some prat's probably dumped a bin bag, too idle to drive to the disposal site. He snaps on his flashlight, walks across.

It's not a bin bag, it's a drunk, one of the Market Square guys. Must've passed out before he could effect entry. Stables touches him with the toe of his boot. 'Come on, sunshine, you can't kip here.' The man doesn't stir so he squats. A few slaps on the cheek'll sometimes do the trick.

Not this time though. As he goes to lift the head he sees it's lying in a puddle of something black. When he points his torch at the puddle it turns out to be dark red, and when he dips a finger in it it's sticky and doesn't smell nice. Constable Stables straightens up, unclips his radio.

For once, Garton Road has turned out not to be a waste of time.

Sixty-seven

Mark slept fitfully in his room on the second floor back and got up when somebody started walking on creaky boards upstairs. He'd no idea of the time, but strong light through the flimsy curtain told him it wasn't ridiculously early. An alcove contained a tiny hand-basin and a smeary mirror in a red plastic frame. He washed in tepid water, dried himself with the threadbare towel and pulled on his clothes, wishing he'd thought to wash his underpants last night. *Probably wouldn't have dried anyway*.

He was hungry. *Straighten bedclothes, open curtain, find*

breakfast. He pulled back the curtain. In the middle distance two policemen were standing by the old boiler. As Mark watched, a ragged man emerged from a sort of doorway in one end of the cylinder and sat among the weeds, knuckling his eyes. A second man appeared, then a third. They got up unsteadily and leaned in a line against the side of the boiler, shielding their eyes from the glare. The policemen were talking, gesturing, pointing. Mark tried to open the window in the hope of hearing what was being said but it was stuck.

After a couple of minutes one of the ragged men detached himself from the boiler, followed a policeman to a patrol car and got in the back. The other policeman stayed a minute talking to the other two, then joined his colleague in the vehicle, which moved off, bouncing over the uneven ground. The ragged men watched it out of sight, then sat down with their backs against the boiler, arms wrapped round knees, faces tilted up to catch the sun. Nothing else seemed likely to happen so Mark locked the door behind him and went out in search of breakfast.

He found Starbucks, ordered coffee and a bagel, sat looking out of the window. It was only half eight, there was hardly anyone in the place. The blonde girl wasn't on duty. He munched and sipped, thinking about his father: how smug the bumptious, self-made windbag must be feeling now that he'd finally acquired Hackers. He could hear the familiar, hectoring voice inside his head saying *'Nobody gets the better of me: nobody. When Ralph Penfold wants a thing, he gets it. Method plus tenacity, that's the secret weapon.'* His long-suffering mother'd be on the receiving end of this stuff as usual, and so would Jess, unless she'd had the sense to go off somewhere till the start of Michaelmas term.

Everything always goes right for you, Father, doesn't it? Falls into your lap. Well not this time. This time there's going to be a hitch. A big one. The sort even you can't fix, and it comes with my compliments. Pity you'll never know that but, still, when it's over, for the first time in my life I'll be dying to see the look on your face.

Breakfast over, he set off to find the skip he'd tossed his bottle into yesterday. There were a couple of items he'd be needing in a few hours' time, and a skip was the perfect place to go looking for them.

Sixty-eight

Dennis woke to the warble of his mobile. *Who the . . .?* He jabbed OK. 'Yeah?'

'Michael. Got the radio on?'

'*This* time of morning? You're joking.'

'It's nearly half-eight, you turkey. Anyway, there's been a murder.'

'Where?'

'What d'you mean, *where*? *Here*, of course: d'you think I'd call you about a murder in Af-sodding-ghanistan? I think it's one of the Circle.'

'Not my *dad*?'

'Oh . . . never thought of that, Den. Sorry. It just said

a homeless man, a familiar figure to shoppers in the town centre.'

'Well it *can't* be my dad then, can it? He only showed up yesterday.'

'No, that's right. Know who *I* think it'll turn out to be?'

'Who?'

'Brasso.'

'What makes you think it's him?'

'Cast your mind back to last Wednesday. What was Brasso doing that isn't generally considered to be a particularly good idea around Midborough?'

Dennis wasn't at his brightest first thing, but he made the effort. 'Ah . . . you mean *Donny Conway*?'

'Exactly, my man. Wednesday, Brasso makes a prat out of Donny Conway, a guy famous for his aversion to being made a prat of, and Saturday a homeless man is found battered to death on the forecourt of a derelict filling-station. Coincidence or what?'

'Phew!' Dennis swung his legs out of bed, reached for his jeans. 'And the police won't know about Brasso's Holy Joe riff, will they?'

'Don't see how.'

'So Donny won't be in the frame.'

'Well, I expect Donny's always *somewhere* in the frame when there's violence in this town, but there's probably nothing to *link* Donny and Brasso, if it *is* Brasso. Nothing the coppers know about, I mean.'

'Which means you . . . *we* have vital information.'

'Right, and we'd better hope Donny Conway doesn't realize that or we'll be next.'

'*Call* 'em, Mike. Call the police: tell 'em about Wednesday and they'll pick Donny up. He can't hurt us if he's in custody.'

'Yeah, but hold on: we don't even know if it *is* Brasso. Tell you what: I'll meet you in half an hour, usual spot, and we'll go down Market Square.'

'What about Tim?'

'I . . . think we'd best leave Tim out of it for now, Den. He'll be scared shitless if he finds out Brasso's dead, and there's always a chance Donny'd nothing to do with it. People kill winos for fun, you know.'

'In America, not here.'

'Hobbies *catch on,* my man: look at skateboards.'

Sixty-nine

Breakfast time, Donny Conway's down the Italia as usual. His appetite isn't good when he's upset, and he's seriously upset this morning. He's ordered his usual meal though, because it's important to act normally. That's why he's speaking quietly to the two minders when he ought to be screaming in their big dumb faces.

'You smegheads,' he hisses, stirring his coffee. 'You brain-dead heaps of festering doggie-doo. I pay you a fortune and you can't be trusted to do anything right.'

The pair look hurt. 'But, Boss,' says one, 'we fixed him just like you said.'

Donny eyeballs him. 'You left it lying around,

pigface. There's a perfectly good river about fifty yards away and you leave the body on a garage forecourt where the first prat who passes is bound to see it.' He puts the spoon on a paper napkin. 'Where's the bat: I suppose you left that for the coppers to find as well, with a label wrapped round it saying BLUNT INSTRUMENT?'

'No, Boss.'

'No, I was forgetting, you can't spell blunt instrument, can you? What did you do with it?'

'Chucked it in the river.'

'Well if you were chucking that in the river, why the bloo . . .' He breaks off, sighs, shakes his head. 'He was a wino, see? A dosser. And the thing about dossers is, they move on. Happens all the time. Nobody asks where they've gone 'cause nobody cares. If you'd slung him in the river, chances are he'd never have been missed. No police involvement. As it is, they're crawling all over the place right now doing fingertip searches, sending bits of this and that to the laboratory where they'll find fibres from your pants and thin hairs from your thick heads. I wouldn't be surprised if one of you dropped a wallet with your address, National Insurance number, blood group and a scrap of paper with a list: COLLECT JACKET FROM CLEANERS, BUY TOOTH-PASTE, KILL DOSSER.'

The minders shake their heads. 'We didn't leave no clues, Boss, honest,' says one.

'Huh!' Donny scoops up a mouthful of cold scrambled egg and talks through it, so that bits spatter the table or land in the men's coffee. 'Only good thing is, the law isn't going to strain itself to find who killed some wino. Blame one of his mates, easiest thing: someone so far gone he won't know whether he did it or not. Now the kid –' He glances all round to make sure nobody can hear – 'the kid's another kettle of fish altogether. I want him, but not like the late reverend. There's no rush, but I want you to keep your eyes skinned, and when he surfaces, which he will, I want him brought you know where, alive and without a mark on him. Without a mark on him. Understand?'

The minders nod. Donny tackles his eggs. Everybody else minds their own business too.

Seventy

'Morning, son.' Jim Clissold looked up from his perch between Digby and Cow. Yomper sat a little apart, staring at the pavement. No Brasso.

'Dad.' He acknowledged his father, looked at Yomper. 'It's true then, Brasso's dead?'

'Oh, aye.'

'They make Yomper hidentify 'im body,' volunteered Cow.

Dennis nodded. Brasso's was his first death: the first time somebody known to him had died. He'd often wondered how it would feel, losing somebody. Grandad, say, or Mam, or if her fall from the slide had killed Marie. He'd assumed some sort of overwhelming emotion –

bewilderment, desolation, anger perhaps – but in fact he was feeling very little. Of course he hadn't known Brasso well, hardly at all really but, still, yesterday the man had been sitting on this wall watching for his mother, and he'd never sit here again. Never. Dennis had never pondered the word 'never': what it actually *meant*. In this case it meant Brasso's absence going on and on and on: a hundred years, a thousand, six hundred million. He tried to get his head round this – the wall crumbling to fragments, the crumbs of brick abraded by rain and wind and frost into dust, the dust becoming overlaid by layer upon layer of debris as Midborough toppled and decayed, vegetation taking root in the debris, growing to a forest, much later, people coming to clear the forest to make way for a settlement, never dreaming that once, long ago, a town stood here. And in time that settlement would become a town, then a city, then the city would begin to crack and fall, and Brasso would *still* be absent. All of this passed through Dennis's mind in a silent half minute, but all it made him feel was a vague dread, a faint giddiness.

'Who d'you think might've done it?' Michael's question, addressed to the Circle generally, brought him out of his reverie.

Digby shook his head. 'Dunno, could be anyone. They'll never get whoever it was.'

'They'll not *try*,' growled Yomper. 'Course, *we* all know who's at the back of it: we just won't say.'

Michael looked at him. 'Who?'

Yomper shook his head. 'Not saying, end up like our mate.'

'You can't just let 'em get away with it.'

Yomper nodded. 'Yes, we can. *I* can anyway. I've had practice.'

'What d'you mean?'

'Hoy!' Digby frowned up at the boy. 'Don't get him started on *that* or we'll have it all day. How about a can, honour of absent friends?'

Michael shook his head. 'No dosh.' It wasn't true, but tonight was going to be special: he'd need every penny.

'You?' Digby stared at Dennis. 'Paid last night, weren't you?'

Dennis shrugged. 'Yes, but I owe my mam . . .'

'Your *mam*?' Jim Clissold sighed, shook his head. 'I *told* you son, you needn't worry about your mam; she's tough. Gets by. Better than the rest of us anyway. Come *on*.' He grinned. 'Hand in pocket, son. 'Tisn't every day we lose a mate and he's looking down, you know, see'f we're missing him.'

'Yes, OK.' Dennis couldn't cry for the dead man but he'd raise a can, they *all* would, and hope it'd do instead. Brasso'd set more store by lager than by tears, and if he ran a bit short there was dead money in Jimmy's piggybank. And Marie's.

Seventy-one

Mark was back in his room at The Railway Hotel by half ten. Somebody had made the bed. He stowed the carrier bag with its two glass bottles and a large plastic milk container in the curtained alcove that served as a wardrobe, dropped the notepad and envelopes he'd bought on the bedside unit.

He crossed to the window but there was nobody near the boiler, no sign of life on the waste ground. He sat on the bed, opened the notepad and wrote 'Dear Sir' at the top of the first page, using the ballpoint with RAILWAY HOTEL printed on it.

Dear Sir

By the time you receive this, the name SIR RALPH PENFOLD will have become topical locally, for a reason you will know. You will understand why I have to remain anonymous, but I promise you that what follows is absolutely true, and might provide an interesting 'angle' on your paper's coverage of an incident, which, at the time of writing, has not occurred: it will certainly give you an exclusive; an opportunity to scoop the nationals.

Sir Ralph Penfold, MD of Penfold Breweries PLC, is a LIFELONG TEETOTALLER. The son of Methodist parents, Sir Ralph was brought up to believe that alcohol is a curse on mankind, uniquely responsible for the destruction of lives and families. When Sir Ralph is seen on public occasions apparently enjoying a glass of the company's product, his glass actually contains cold tea or sometimes grape juice. This has been a closely guarded secret, known only to his family and a handful of trusted friends. (This letter is proof that trust is sometimes misplaced!) I wish that it were possible for me to furnish proof of my allegation, but it is not. However, I suspect it will

not be too difficult for a journalist to uncover the truth, now s/he has the scent.
Yours sincerely,
A friend of truth

It goes without saying that Mark did not produce this letter at the first attempt. By the time it was done to his satisfaction seven pages of false starts and crossings-out lay screwed up on the floor. He printed the address of Midborough's evening paper on an envelope, slipped the folded letter inside and sealed it. He didn't put a stamp on. His route this evening would take him right past the newspaper's offices: he'd deliver it by hand.

He'd printed both letter and envelope, using his left hand. The result was untidy but untraceable back to him, or so he hoped. He propped the envelope against the phone, gathered the screwed-up sheets of paper and dumped them in the washbasin, making sure he'd got them all. The stationer's receipt went in too. Producing a disposable lighter, he set fire to the papers, poking them about as they burned so that no scrap remained uncharred. When only ashes were left he crumbled them to powder with his fingers and ran the tap till everything had swirled off down the plughole.

This done, he took the pad and the remaining envelopes to the curtained alcove and dropped them in the carrier with the bottles. He looked round the room, satisfying himself that no evidence remained of his having written a letter in it. There was a burnt-paper smell, but since the window wouldn't open he'd have to let it disperse in its own time.

His preparations complete, he lay down on the bed and closed his eyes. This was going to be the hardest part: waiting for dark, trying not to think too much about what he'd set himself to do tonight.

Holding his nerve.

Seventy-two

'What're you getting dolled up for, our Dennis?' Eight o'clock. Dennis was fixing his hair, hogging the bathroom. His mother had toiled upstairs with a stack of freshly ironed clothes for the airing cupboard.

''S OK, Mam, you can come in. I've just about finished.'

She stood behind him, shelving shirts. 'Off out?'

'Yeah, meeting Tim and Michael. Did I tell you I saw Dad?'

'You told me twice: last night and this afternoon. Your memory's getting as bad as his.'

'It's not that, Mam: you didn't say owt. I thought maybe you didn't hear me.'

'I heard you. Both times. Smelt you as well, but I've nothing to say about your father except I hope he isn't encouraging you to drink more than you do already.'

'Course not. He asked about you and the kids.'

'Huh! Lot *he* cares. You want to stay away from him, our Dennis: Jim Clissold and swotting for re-sits don't mix. And while we're on the subject of re-sits, don't go frittering your wages away, clubbing. Re-sits cost fifteen pounds per subject, and you needn't think *I'm* going to pay: if you've to find the fees yourself you'll mebbe take it more seriously.'

Dennis lowered the comb, tilted his head, admired the effect. 'I'm taking it seriously anyway, Mam. We *all* are. Tonight's like one last fling before we turn ourselves into monks or hermits or something.'

His mother closed the cupboard door, sighed. 'I *want* to believe that, Dennis, but I'm finding it hard. It's the sort of thing your father used to say and you've seen where *he* ended up.'

'I'm not Dad, Mam: I'm *me*. You'll never catch me sitting on a wall with a bottle in a paper bag.'

She turned, caught his eye in the mirror. 'You fail those re-sits, lad, and it won't matter to me *where* you go: you won't be *here*, that's all I know.'

She left the bathroom. Dennis swallowed, wishing she hadn't said that. Bit of a damper on his mood. He gazed at his reflection, murmured, 'Hear that, did you, you mammal? Last time, so make the most of it. Go out there and knock their socks off.'

He meant girls, but he didn't mean socks.

Seventy-three

'Timothy, my man: you *made* it.'

'I said I was coming.'

'Yeah, but you sounded like . . . dubious.'

'*You'd* be dubious in my shoes, you pachyderm. Donny's not looking for *you.*'

Michael pulled a face. 'You don't know he's looking for *you*: could be a coincidence, Brasso getting the chop just now. Anyway.' He grinned. 'Where's safer than Hackers? Sort of guys work for Donny'd never get past the door staff.'

'You wouldn't be so laid-back if –'

'Ah, *here* he is.' Michael beamed as Dennis appeared. 'Nice timing, Den.'

Dennis shrugged, didn't smile. Marie's tens and fifties weighed heavy in his pocket. 'Hadn't we better get in the queue: Nick Rafferty'll pull 'em in.' Nick Rafferty was guest DJ tonight.

Michael nodded. 'Well up-market: new owner's making it happen, guys.'

'Well up-*price* and all,' grumbled Tim as the trio started walking. 'I'd rather pay the old six quid, dance to D-trick Fissure Disco: always good enough for me.'

Michael grinned. 'You're a miserable bleeder, Timothy. Donny shows up, no prob: you'll *depress* him to death.'

They walked up Infirmary Road. Tim's eyes were

everywhere till Bridge Street, which was so busy he felt able to relax. Nobody would be stupid enough to make a hit in front of all these witnesses.

Dennis had been right: the queue was much longer than usual. The trio tagged on at ten-thirty and it was ten to eleven before they made the lobby. 'Certs at the ready, guys,' murmured Michael, but the door staff hadn't changed and they passed unchallenged.

Paul Van Dyk was blitzing the place with *The Riddle*. The dance floor was packed. They shoved their way to the bar. Red Bulls were two-sixty, up ten, could've been worse. They knocked them back, got more, stood watching the lights that seemed brighter, more complex. They sipped their booze and started to sway, minds and bodies seguing into the beat. Hang-ups withered, sloughed off and were left behind. *Why do I get uptight . . . why does* anybody, *when it could be like this all the time if you'd just . . . let it* take *you*.

Time passed, in no time. Dennis had got a bottle of water from somewhere, he couldn't remember. He let it hang, holding it by the neck as he danced, facing a girl he knew from school. She was beautiful. Not just looks: a beautiful *person*, swaying against a background of other beautiful people. He wondered vaguely where all these people were the *rest* of the week: you never met one on the bus, did you, or in a shop? Nothing but miseries out there. *I wanna live here with these people for ever: the permanent high.*

'Fancy topping up?' She was talking to him. *Karen, was it? Sharon?*

He frowned. 'Topping up?'

'Yeah, you *know*.' She mimed popping something in her mouth, swallowing. 'Come on.'

Well, why not?

It was the toilet. Women's toilet. He expected she'd go in, do the deal, he'd wait here. He fumbled for his wallet. She stopped his hand with one of her own, smiling. 'Come on, it's all right.'

White tiles, bright lights. Girls at mirrors. He hung back. 'I don't think . . .'

'It's cool, Den, look: nobody's squealing.' Nobody was. She took his hand, led him to a cubicle, locked the door. It was sparkling, fragrant, not like a toilet at all. More like . . .

'Watch.' She faced him, pulled up her top. He thought, *This is it. This is really, really* it.

It was.

Seventy-four

Getting it in wasn't easy: the hole was tiny, he'd never done it before and his nervousness didn't help. Luckily nobody was watching, and at the third attempt the nozzle went in and he squeezed the lever.

It was a two-litre milk container. There was no cap, so when it was full he bunged the opening with tissues and carried it into the pay-station-cum-shop, trying to look like somebody who's trudged quite a way. He'd concocted a story about his dad's car having run dry a

mile back but he needn't have bothered: the sole atten-
dant was trying to watch something on TV and clearly
found customers irritating. 'Number four? One sixty-six.
Receipt?'

'No thanks.' He gave her two, she dumped change in
his palm and turned immediately to the guy behind,
impatient to clear the place. Mark picked up the container and left. As far as he could tell, nobody had taken
the slightest notice of him or his unusual purchase.
Couldn't have worked out better.

He re-crossed the road, retrieved the plastic carrier
from the litterbin he'd dropped it in and walked away.
As he crossed Market Square the clock above the
jeweller's was showing nine-o-five. It would be silly to
return to the hotel, then go out again pretty late. Sort of
thing that draws attention. Besides, he was starting to
feel jumpy, in need of a drink. He hadn't much money:
eleven pounds and some change. Enough for a can or
two anyway. He crossed to Thresher.

Seventy-five

The heat evaporated Tim's cares and the beat blew them
away. If somebody had leaned in and hissed '*Donny
Conway*' he'd have said '*Who?*' And if Rafferty had
inserted the word '*re-sits*' into his rap (as if) he'd have
thought, *Re-sits: what're they?* Tim was happy. Tim was
dancing. Tim was high.

Michael was doing all right too, but one thing was irritating him. The new regime at Hackers had set on some new security staff who didn't know the meaning of low profile. There were two guys, and they were in your face all the time: patrolling the floor, peering at you and getting in the way. They hadn't grabbed anybody yet, but they were obviously dead keen and when you're under age and under this sort of scrutiny it does your head in, messes up the mood.

Tim, surfing the sub bass, didn't notice till someone grabbed his shoulder. He shrugged himself free and turned, and the bouncer mouthed something he couldn't hear for the music. 'What?' He *knew* what: he wasn't wrecked or violent so it had to be his age. The guy mouthed something that might have been '*Come on*' and jerked his head towards the door. Tim looked for Dennis and Michael but couldn't spot them. Seeing no alternative he made an apologetic face at the girl he'd been dancing with and started to follow the bouncer. The DJ picked that instant to rewind and in the split second's break Tim heard the guy say what sounded like, 'Donny's pretty pissed . . .'

Donny. Terror's a downer, Tim hit bottom. The bouncer wasn't actually holding him so he whirled and barged across the middle of the floor, pursued by cries of 'Oi!' from outraged dancers. He'd no goal in mind except to put a few precious metres between himself and Donny's minder. If the guy had done club work before, or had had a few more brain cells he'd have caught the boy in seconds. If he hadn't been getting up everybody's nose, people might have moved aside and let him through instead of obstructing him. As it was, a combination of circumstances enabled Tim to reach the wall and swerve right, heading for the toilets. His plan, if you could call it that, was to go in the women's. The bouncer might hesitate before barging in there, long enough for him to lock himself in a cubicle anyway. There'd be other locked cubicles and the guy wouldn't know which door to kick in. It wasn't much of a plan, but it was the best he could manage on the run.

He burst through the door. Dennis, straightening his jacket in a mirror, winked at him. 'Gonna do it sitting down, Tim?'

Seventy-six

In other circumstances Tim might've taken a few seconds to ask what the heck his friend was doing here, but he didn't have any to spare. 'Donny's guy,' he gasped, nodding towards the door. 'Gotta hide.'

Dennis's encounter with Karen had heightened his perceptions and left him feeling sharp, which was lucky. 'Here.' He grabbed Tim's sleeve, tugging him towards the cubicle he'd recently vacated and from which Karen was even now emerging, smoothing her skirt. At the height of the fun he'd looked up and noticed a displaced ceiling-panel directly over the cubicle and it had crossed his mind that Karen might have somebody up there taking pictures. He hadn't seriously thought so, of course, and if he *had* he wouldn't have cared at the time, but that's why he thought of it now. Knocking Karen sideways he pulled Tim into the cubicle and indicated the rectangular opening. 'Up there,' he rapped, sliding home the doorbolt.

Tim sprang on to the seat, grabbed the top of the partition and planted one shoe in Dennis's cupped hands. Dennis heaved upwards, propelling his friend's head and shoulders into darkness. Tim's groping hands found a strut of rough timber. He grabbed it and hauled himself into the crawlspace between the old, high ceiling and the new one. 'Panel!' hissed Dennis. Kneeling, Tim slid the square of tacboard into place, leaving himself in near-total darkness. As he did so the women's room door swung open and the bouncer walked in.

Karen, who hadn't a clue what was happening, stood gawping as the man strode along the row of cubicles kicking doors open. As he reached the one concealing Dennis she cried, 'Hey, my friend's in there.'

The bouncer glared at her. 'See a boy come in, did you?'

'*Boy?* Why would a boy . . .?'

'Did you *see* one?' he shouted.

'No.' She shook her head. 'There's just me and . . . Denise.'

'You *sure?*'

'Course.'

'Huh!' He glanced about suspiciously as though somebody might be hiding in the hand-drier, then spun on his heel and walked out.

Dennis heard the door, hissed, 'Karen?'

'What?' She hadn't forgotten how he'd shoved her aside.

'Has he gone?'

'Yes.'

He came out, looked at her. 'I heard what you said to him, Karen. Thanks.'

''S all right, but what the *heck* . . .?' She indicated the ceiling panel.

Dennis nodded. 'I'll explain, but not here. Just a sec.' He stood under the panel. 'Tim?'

'Yeah?'

'Stay there till the music stops at two. Everybody'll be leaving. Slip out and mingle. Guy can't watch everyone, and anyway he'll assume you left ages ago. We'll wait outside.'

'What's the time now? I can't see a thing up here.'

'It's five to one.'

'OK.'

Karen opened the door, took a peek. Nobody was watching. They slipped out and Dennis steered her towards the chill-out room. Seventies, low volume. They sat down.

Karen looked at him. 'OK, *Denise*,' she murmured, 'shoot.'

Seventy-seven

Trance had elevated Michael to a plane where bouncers and the world they move in either don't exist or don't matter. There was a girl dancing topless; not with him but near enough to qualify as a close encounter of the third kind, so he was mightily hacked off when Dennis jerked into focus, gurning and gesticulating.

'*What?*' he grated, as his friend (ex-friend?) led him into the chill-out room where Gary Numan was asking whether friends are electric. They joined some girl at a table. Briefly, Dennis filled Michael in on what had happened, which brought him down fast. 'So one of Donny's heavies is *here?*'

Dennis nodded. 'It's one of the new security guys.' He indicated the girl. 'Karen saw him.'

Michael acknowledged her with a nod, looked at Dennis. 'If Donny's after Tim, it means it *was* him killed Brasso, right?'

'Probably.'

'Well look, I've got my mobile. Why don't I call the police, tell 'em we know who did it? Roomful of cops, guy'll be too busy fudging his shorts to bother about Tim.'

Dennis shook his head. 'Sounds OK but it isn't and I'll tell you why. One: call comes from some kid in a club at one in the morning, probably wrecked on vodka, pills. What cop's going to take it seriously? Two: we're under age, alcohol in the blood if nothing else. Cops *do* come, *we're* the ones arrested, Hackers could get closed down, bouncer walks away. No, I say we leave it like it is, see Tim outside, work out something to tell the police tomorrow.'

Michael frowned. 'So why drag me off the floor, my man? I was *flying!*'

Dennis shrugged. 'Sorry. Thought you'd want to know where Tim is, that's all, what's happening.' He looked at his watch. 'You've fifty minutes, time to get back into it.'

Michael got up, looked down at his friend. 'You not coming?'

Dennis shook his head. 'Me and Karen got a dance of our own, one of the smaller floors.'

Karen giggled.

Seventy-eight

Bins and bottles, mused Mark. *For the would-be Master of Meldilorn, it's all come down to bins and bottles.*

He was sitting on cobbles in the dank yard at the rear of Hackers, his back against the wall. Two wheelie-bins stood between him and the loading-bay, the four windows. Around him on the ground stood nine bottles, seven of them empty. Six of the empties were beer bottles. German pils, six for four-ninety at Thresher. The other empty was a two-litre milk container that reeked of petrol. The petrol was now in two glass milk-bottles he'd found in the skip. He'd bunged their necks with the ripped-out sleeves of the T-shirt he had on, which showed how wrecked he was on the six-pack.

Two bins, nine bottles.

He'd no way of knowing the time, but it had been dark for ages and his bum was numb so it must be late.

The venue's thumping bass was easily audible from here: when it stopped, his time would come to act. Part of him was impatient for this, part was not.

'It is a bah, bah fetter thing that I do,' he slurred for the umpteenth time, 'than I have ever done; it is a far, far fetter resht that I go to, than I have ever known.' He giggled. *It is the best thing isn't it . . . not sure about the rest, though. Can't guillotine me, even if they catch me. Prison's a sort of rest, I suppose . . .*

He jerked his head up, frowned. What's that, what's *happening*? Then he recognized silence.

'Shit!' He shifted stiffly, drew up his legs, rocked on to one numb buttock, tottered upright. *Two o'clock: they're pouring out, grabbing taxis. Nobody wants to hang around once the music stops. Say ten minutes, then watch the windows. Lights go out, staff's away. Couple of minutes, let 'em get clear, then it's all systems go. No casualties except Sir Ralph's gigantic ego, his bottomless pocket. Pray God he's not insured.*

He leaned on the wall, toying with the disposable lighter, watching the windows through the gap between the bins.

Seventy-nine

'Where the heck *is* he?' grumbled Michael, 'I want my bed.'

'Quit moaning, you camel.' Dennis's plan to share a

taxi with Karen had had to be abandoned. She'd hung around a bit, tutting and looking at her watch before taking a cab with three girls she knew. *Didn't even wave.*

It was half past two. All the taxis had gone. Clubbers as well, except the two of them. And Tim, wherever he was. They'd crossed the road, not wanting to be obviously loitering when the staff came out. Now lights were being switched off inside, figures gathering in the lobby. A taxi drew up. The bar staff came out, two girls and a guy. They got in the cab and were whisked away.

Michael shook his head. 'He must've snook out with the plonkers who leave early to grab taxis.'

'If he'd done that,' murmured Dennis, 'he'd have been here waiting for us. I told him we'd see him outside.'

'Yeah, but he's scared: probably didn't fancy hanging about where Donny's guy might spot him.'

'No,' insisted Dennis, 'what's happened is he's left it too late, gonna be locked in.'

Michael sighed. 'So *then* what, my man?'

Dennis shrugged. 'Dunno. Depends if he can find a way out. Door might open easily from inside, or he could try round the back.'

'There'll be *alarms*, dummy. Second he starts moving about in there, all hell'll break loose.'

'*So?* What d'you think *I* can do about it? Sod off if you want, Michael: *I'm* not leaving him.'

They gazed across Bridge Street. Two cars. Four men came out of Hackers, got in one, drove off. The lobby lights dipped to a dim glow and three guys came out. One stayed, fiddling with locks, while the others got in the vehicle. They watched him try the door, then turn and cross to the car. The driver started up and the car pulled away, heading towards Infirmary Road. As the two boys stepped out of the shadow they'd lurked in there came a crash of breaking glass, followed at once by another. It seemed to come from the alley at the side of the club. Dennis shot Michael a look of triumph. 'What did I *tell* you?' he crowed. 'He's out.'

Eighty

Michael had been right: there *were* alarms. Their shrill beeping splintered the night as the two boys pelted across the road. *If it's one of those systems connected direct to a police station,* thought Dennis as they groped blindly along the alley, *they'll be here in a minute.* He'd nothing against the police: had a story to tell them in fact, but if they showed up right now to find a smashed window and three lads in the yard, he doubted they'd listen. *Hope there's a back way out.*

'Look!' gasped Michael. The darkness ahead was becoming suffused with a faint orange glow against which the corner of the building was visible. 'I think the place is on fire.'

'No!' The glow pulsated, growing brighter till they could see where they were putting their feet. They spurted, burst on to the cobbled yard.

Shards of glass glinted on the cobbles. Looking up, the

boys saw four windows, one above another. The first and third of these were broken, their glassless woodwork framing flames that leapt and crackled, their snapping audible over the alarm's relentless wail. The glow illuminated every corner of the yard, and nobody was there.

'Tim!' Dennis stared at the windows, seeking movement that wasn't smoke or flame. 'Come on, Tim, get *out* of there.'

Michael touched his sleeve. 'He'll have *got* out, Den, the second he smashed the window. We were across the road, remember.'

Dennis, frantic, indicated the yard with a sweep of his arm. 'Where *is* he then?'

'He'll have got over the wall.'

'Why *two* windows, Michael, one too high to jump?'

'I . . . dunno. *Heat*. Heat broke the high one, it does that.'

Without taking his gaze away from the windows, Dennis shook his head. 'Heat broke 'em *both*, Michael. The fire started by itself and he's *in* there.' He swung round, cheeks shiny with tears. 'Why the heck would he set the place on *fire*, you turkey. Get on your mobile, fire brigade, do it NOW!'

Eighty-one

Tim hadn't gone over the wall but Mark had, dropping into the narrow street beyond as Dennis and Michael stumbled up the alley. Hammered though he was he'd brought everything with him in the plastic carrier; had left no telltale clue. Nor had he gone far. No need and no point. This was a commercial section of Midborough: no houses, nobody about this time of night, no danger of being seen. And where's the satisfaction in torching something belonging to a tyrant if you're not there to watch it burn?

He'd crossed the street, found another yard with bins and clambered into a giant wheelie that happened to be empty. Good, that. Made him laugh out loud. Or was the glow in the sky responsible? Didn't matter.

It wasn't long before he heard sirens. Not long *enough* really because he wanted the place gutted. Smoke damage wouldn't do, water damage. Total destruction, that was the ticket.

He needn't have worried. Michael had failed to get a signal in the yard, had had to sprint back down the alleyway on to Bridge Street and call from there. By the time the first appliance arrived, the second floor had collapsed, carrying the floors beneath it into the cellar where the spirits were stored, with some cylinders of gas under pressure. It was better than bonfire night.

Mark had a grandstand view. One appliance came round the back. Its crew couldn't get the big wooden gates open so they set about it with axes and crowbars. Mark knelt on the floor of the bin, propping its hinged lid with his head to leave a slot he could watch through. It was really interesting. The gates yielded at last and the appliance was manoeuvred halfway into the yard. Hoses were deployed, jets of water arced on to the club's smoking roof and turned to steam but it was too late: the roof fell in anyway, flinging shoals of sparks at the sky.

Mark cheered.

Eighty-two

'Our mate's in there!'

'Eh?' The fireman frowned, busy with the hydrant, half-deafened by sirens.

Dennis grabbed his sleeve, pointed. 'There's a lad in there, over the toilets, gorra gerrimout.'

'Over the toilets? What you *on* about, son?' *Been popping* pills, *haven't you? Course you have.*

'Guy was after him, he hid above the toilets. Tim. Tim Broadbent.'

The man glanced up, saw the kid was crying, grabbed his sleeve. 'You telling me there's somebody inside that building?'

'Yes, I've been trying –'

'But the place was *closed*, how . . .?' A man was hurrying by. 'Sir?' The man stopped and the fireman indicated Dennis. 'Kid says there's someone inside, sir.'

The man frowned at Dennis. 'Was it you called us?'

'Yes. Well, my mate did.' *What's it* matter, *for chrissake* – Tim's *in there.*

'And how do you know there's somebody inside, lad?'

―''Cause *I* gave him a leg-up, into the ceiling: why don't you *do* something, you donkey.'

'That's *enough*, young man.' The guy pointed. 'Over there: take your pal with you and keep out of the way. *We'll* deal with this.'

The police had arrived. *Over there* was a section of pavement they'd cordoned off to keep sightseers back. The two boys trudged across, joined a handful of nosy citizens gawping at the blaze past the shoulders of five big constables. Four fire-fighters went in through the front door wearing breathing apparatus. An ambulance wailed up the street, a PC flagged it down. Almost at once three of the fire-fighters reappeared, supporting the fourth. They laid him on the wet tarmac. The ambulance crew hurried forward with a stretcher, lifted the fire-fighter on to it and carried him to their vehicle. The second its doors closed the ambulance pulled out, did a U-turn and sped away, its blue lights flashing.

Dennis followed it with stricken eyes, stretched out an arm as if to call it back. 'Hey!' he croaked. 'What about . . . wait for . . .' He gazed at Michael, who shook his head. 'Let it go, Den: Tim doesn't need it now.'

Eighty-three

Something wakes Susan Clissold: a dream perhaps, or a sixth sense. Dennis? She lifts her head, peers at the clock on the bedside unit. Two thirty-five. In the distance there are sirens, perhaps they woke her? Dennis though: why Dennis?

She slips out of bed, pads barefoot along the landing, peeps into his room. The duvet's unrumpled: he's still out. She goes to the bathroom, then back to her bedroom but not to bed. When Marie had that fall in the park, Susan had known. Not in detail: just a feeling one of the kids was in trouble. She has that feeling now.

She goes to the window, parts the curtains, sees the fire. No flames from here, just a glow reflected off the undersides of clouds. Must be pretty big to do that, I wonder . . .

A memory: years ago in the Channel Islands, or was it the Isle of Man? A night club anyway, hundreds burned to death. It was in all the papers.

Susan's vague unease congeals to cold certainty. She grabs her dressing-gown, hurries downstairs, approaches the phone.

Who d'you call, fire brigade, police? She's no idea: who do you ask about a fire in the middle of the night?

The *Gazette*, try the *Gazette*: they'll know but will they tell me, and is anybody there at night? It's only a local paper. She riffles through the directory, finds the number, stabs buttons.

'Newsdesk.'

'Oh, hello: I'm hoping you can help me. There seems to be a building on fire in town, d'you know about it?'

'Uh . . . yes we do, thanks. Got a man at the scene: photographer. Appreciate your calling though: we –'

'Where is it, is it Hackers? My son was going there and he hasn't come home.'

'I . . . I'm really not the person to talk to about this, love. The police –'

'Please, just tell me if it's Hackers.'

'OK, yes it is, but I understand the fire broke out after the place closed for the night so you mustn't worry . . .'

'Thanks.' She hangs up and sits with the directory open across her lap, staring at the floor. She never prays – doesn't believe in God – but she's talking to somebody: making promises.

'Let our Dennis be safe. Send him home and I swear I'll never threaten to throw him out again. Never, never, never . . .'

Eighty-four

As the phone rings in the newsroom of the *Midborough Gazette*, another rings in Sir Ralph's bedroom. He wakes up, picks up. 'Penfold.'

'Cargill, Sir Ralph.' Cargill manages Hackers. He's been in the job three weeks. 'I'm sorry to call at this time of night but I thought you'd want to know. The police just rang; apparently the club's on fire.'

'What?' Sir Ralph swings his legs out of bed, hunches forward, runs his free hand through what's left of his hair. 'What d'you mean, on fire? Is it bad? What do they say?'

'It sounds pretty bad, I'm afraid, Sir Ralph. I'm on

my way there now. I'll call you the minute I know anything.'

'You needn't bother.'

He's on his feet, reaching for clothes as Lady Jane blinks and mumbles, 'What is it, dear? Is it Mark?'

'I'm on my way.' He hangs up, glares at his wife. 'No, it isn't Mark, you obsessed hag. Why should everything be Mark lately?'

It is though, in a way.

Eighty-five

Three a.m. Susan at the front door, frantic. She's phoned the infirmary: they've admitted a fire-fighter, no Dennis Clissold. For the first time since he left, she misses her husband. Jim never actually did anything but he was always calm; wouldn't let things get to him. 'Stop fretting, love,' he'd have said in this situation, 'he'll turn up, you'll see.'

Something moves under the lamp down the road. Susan's heart kicks but she daren't let herself hope. Hope's a wonderful thing, but it doesn't half hurt when it's dashed. Cat, most likely.

She watches the gap between next-door's privet hedge and the fence next door but one. Something crosses the gap and there are footsteps. 'Dennis?'

'Mam . . . oh, Maaam.' He's sobbing, reaching for her like the child he was as he staggers up the path.

Their arms go round each other. Both are weeping: she from relief. 'Tim,' chokes Dennis. 'Tim, Tim, Tim.' She rocks him without knowing the reason for his distress: not ready to know just yet.

Later, inside, with the door closed and dawn at the window, it comes out. 'My fault, Mam,' he sobs, 'I shoved him up there, left him. If I hadn't . . .'

'Ssssh.' She holds her son. 'You did what you had to do, our Dennis. You couldn't know there'd be a fire. Tim wouldn't want you to blame yourself, you know he wouldn't. It was an accident.' She thinks, *his poor mother*, but can't stop a part of herself thinking, *rather her than me*.

She'll phone her in the morning, say something that's meant to comfort, but won't. Of course it won't. In the meantime there's Dennis to see to. 'There's Dennis,' she murmurs, so softly he doesn't hear, and adds, 'Thank you.'

Eighty-six

'Michael? Dennis.'

'Oh, hi.'

'Did I wake you?'

'Yeah, what time is it?'

'Sorry. It's half nine. We've got to talk to the police: sooner the better, I thought.'

'I know, I was thinking about that last night and it's not just Brasso: they killed Tim as well.'

'With help from me.'

'Huh? How d'you *mean*, help from you?'

'*I* told him to hide up there. If I hadn't . . .'

'If you hadn't, that bouncer would have got him and either done him in on the spot or turned him over to Donny Conway, which comes to the same thing. Either way, it's down to Donny so yeah: what time d'you want to meet?'

'Eleven, usual place?'

'Fine. See you there.'

'See you.'

'Yes, what can we do for you?' The constable had to stoop to look through the hatch.

'We've got some information about the murder,' said Michael.

'Oh aye: what murder's this then?'

'The wino. Brasso, he was called.'

'Was he now? And what's this information you've got, lad?'

'We know who did it, or had it done. Know *why* as well.'

'You're having me on, yeah?'

'No.' Dennis shook his head. 'Our mate Tim Broadbent, right? He was in trouble with Donny Conway, and Brasso . . .'

'Whoa!' The lanky constable stopped him, treated both boys to a quizzical look. 'Tim Broadbent? Donny Conway?' He slid a thick pad towards himself. 'I'll take your names and a few details, fetch someone.'

The detective sergeant led them to an interview

room, gave them chairs, gazed at them across a table. 'Right-o then. Who wants to kick us off?'

'I will,' volunteered Michael.

The sergeant nodded. 'From the beginning, lad.'

Michael told the detective how Tim had borrowed twenty pounds belonging to his dad's bowling club, then had to borrow from Donny the moneylender to pay it back. He told how the interest on the loan mounted to a point where Tim couldn't possibly find the money, and how scared the boy had been because Donny's ruthlessness towards those who couldn't pay was common knowledge. He went on to tell of Brasso's intervention on Tim's behalf, as Brasso had told it to the group on the wall in Market Square. 'He went up the Italia, called himself the Reverend Nicholas Cribb, asked Donny to let Tim off.' Michael shrugged. 'Donny agreed, but we reckon he found out Brasso'd made a prat out of him and had him killed.'

'Hmmm.' The sergeant nodded. 'And this Tim Broadbent: he's the same Tim Broadbent whose body was recovered this morning at the scene of the club fire?'

Michael nodded, staring at the table. 'Dennis knows about that, he'd better tell you.'

In other circumstances Dennis would have been embarrassed at having to admit he'd been in the women's toilet at Hackers last night, but as things were it didn't seem to matter. He told how he'd been at the mirror, straightening his hair when Tim burst in saying, 'Donny's guy.' He explained about the displaced ceiling-panel, and how he'd boosted his friend into the space. At this point he filled up and couldn't continue, and the sergeant had a glass of water brought in and told him to take his time. After a minute or two he got a hold of himself and went on. 'The guy came in. I was still in the cubicle so I didn't see him: just heard his voice when he spoke to Karen, but I'd noticed him earlier because he was new, and because he was so in your face on the dance floor.'

'And you're saying there's a connection between this man and Donny Conway?'

'I think so. Tim called him "Donny's guy", but I don't know how *he* knew.'

'Maybe,' interrupted Michael, 'the guy mentioned Donny to Tim when he tried to grab him.'

The sergeant nodded. 'That's possible. Anyway.' He stood up. 'You've both been extremely helpful. I'm really sorry about your friend, but if it turns out you're right about our Mr Conway, it won't be long before he pays for what he did.'

They had to put their statements in writing and sign them. When they got outside it was half twelve and raining. They ducked into Burger King and got Cokes, but when the time came to order food they found they had no appetite. They sat watching raindrops run down the window, thinking the sort of thoughts that never get put into words.

Eighty-seven

While Dennis and Michael are busy at the police station, a skeleton crew of fire-fighters is on damping-down duty round what's left of Hackers. There's a police presence, partly because of the boy's body and partly because there's some concern over how the fire started. There's been an owner presence too, but Sir Ralph has finally run out of bluster and gone home, to the relief of all concerned.

In a way it's a shame the great man hasn't stuck around, because fifteen minutes after his departure a fire-fighter tidying up round the back opens a wheelie bin to dispose of some splinters from the wrecked gate and finds Sir Ralph's son curled up in the bottom, fast asleep. The fire-fighter doesn't know who the lad is, and ordinarily would simply rouse him and tell him to make himself scarce, but there's a strong whiff of petrol as the lid goes up, traceable to an empty milk container in the sleeper's plastic carrier. Police are summoned and the youth, who seems confused and gives his name as Charles Seward, is helped into a patrol car and whisked away to help with inquiries.

Donny Conway is packing a few things for a sudden trip when the front door of his barn conversion is blasted from its hinges and the room is suddenly full of armed policemen. When cautioned, he tells the detective sergeant he's never heard of anybody called Stephen King, unless the sergeant means the famous American author. The nickname Brasso doesn't ring any bells either, and as for the Reverend Nicholas Cribb, Donny claims he's had no contact with a Reverend since his christening in 1959.

Unfortunately for the moneylender, one of his minders has already been questioned and has confessed to having watched a colleague club the wino to death on Donny's orders. He's also confessed to having been on bouncer duty at Hackers last night when the same colleague tried to apprehend a certain young man, also on Donny's instructions. 'Bit hasty, old Travis,' the minder says on tape, 'don't know his own strength.' When the sergeant tells Donny all this, the moneylender cries.

For the first time since his christening in 1959.

Eighty-eight

The *Gazette* carries a front-page picture of the blaze at its height, and a banner headline which reads 'DEATH OF TRAGIC TIM – POLICE BAFFLED'. But it's Monday's paper, which is really packed with dynamite.

'DRUNKEN SON TORCHED TT FATHER'S FLAGSHIP', runs the headline. 'TRAGIC TIM "VICTIM OF DEBT AND VENDETTA".'

The story under this headline is complicated. It includes a number of names, some well-known, some about to become so. It describes Mark (alias Charles Seward) as 'son of booze tycoon Sir Ralph Penfold,' and tells of his arrest and subsequent confession on being told of Tim's death. It quotes Mark's letter to the *Gazette*, with its startling revelation of his father's secret, and goes on to explore the alleged link between Tim and Donny Conway who, together with four employees, is helping police with their inquiries. Among other names mentioned are those of the late Stephen King (aka Brasso, Major Henshaw, Lars Pedersen, Ernest Lawson and Reverend Nicholas Cribb) Dennis Clissold, Michael Houldsworth and Marigold Westhouse.

It will be weeks, perhaps months, before the chickens in all of this come home to roost but when they do, the consequences will be these:

Mark Penfold will be deemed to have fled the Abbeyfield School after a nervous breakdown: a condition under whose influence all of his subsequent actions were carried out. He will go into a clinic where, after some months of treatment, he will recover from both the breakdown and his dependency on alcohol. He will re-establish contact with his parents, but will never live with them again.

Mocked in the tabloids as the TT Tipple Tycoon, Sir Ralph Penfold will resign as MD of Penfold Breweries plc, put Garton Hall on the market and move with the long-suffering Lady Jane to Portugal, where he will grow fond of that country's red wine and become a far nicer person.

Donny Conway will be tried, found guilty of procuring the murder of Brasso and jailed for life. Travis the minder will get fifteen years. Seventy-seven hard-up citizens of Midborough, their debts miraculously written off, will walk on air.

Marigold Westhouse, slated by sections of the press for having harboured an under-age fugitive, will be comforted by Charles Seward and will marry him. The couple will continue to employ Susan in spite of her frequent mutterings about Charles Manson and what people must expect if they're daft enough to take strange young men into their homes.

There'll be no happy ending for Cow, Yomper and Digby. Jim Clissold will take Brasso's place on the wall in Market Square and the Midborough Wine Circle will continue to meet till one by one its members succumb to madness, disease or hypothermia.

Eighty-nine

Four-fifteen on a raw November afternoon. Dennis Clissold comes up the garden path, blowing into cold hands. Distantly, unseasonably, sounds the chime of an ice-cream van. Three weeks of two-hour exam papers have left Dennis feeling shattered, but today's has been the last and he walks with a spring in his step.

His mother is peeling potatoes at the sink. She looks up as he comes in. 'How d'you think it went, our

Dennis?' She's asked this question nine times in twenty days and has received the answer she hears now. 'Doddle, Mam: A-star, no danger.'

'Good, good.' She smiles, hardly daring to believe the evidence of her eyes and ears. She's watched him study solidly for three months, never going out except to work at Wicklow's or revise at the library. To her knowledge he hasn't taken so much as a sip of lager in all that time. He seems to have put Tim's death behind him. He's bright-eyed, sharp, confident.

He hangs his jacket over the newel-post, bounds upstairs with his backpack. His mother's smile has brought back Teresa Summerscales's words: *Don't take her sunshine away.* He grins. *Nosy trollop needn't have worried, right?*

Jimmy comes out of the bathroom, frowns at his brother. 'What *you* grinning at, pizza-face?' Dennis is cultivating a sprinkling of zits, hence the nickname.

He shakes his head, feeling too cool to slap the kid's ear. 'None of your flipping business, you misshapen tunnel-dwarf.' Jimmy sticks out his tongue and scampers downstairs.

Dennis goes into his room, throws his pack in a corner and opens the window, filling his lungs with cold, clean air. He feels focused, capable. Against his father's advice he stands with his eyes closed, picturing.

'Mam?' Jimmy enters the kitchen. 'Can I have one-pound fifty for me and Marie for some ice-cream?'

Susan shakes her head. 'It isn't ice-cream weather, and anyway it's too near dinnertime.'

'Aw, *Ma*-am,' whines Marie, '*let* him, *please*: we could stick it in the freezer for after.'

Their mother sighs. It *isn't* ice-cream weather and it *is* too near dinnertime, but Dennis has put her in a rare good mood and anyway, they aren't kids long. 'All right, then.' She fishes the coins out of her purse, gives them to Jimmy. 'You go, our Marie stays here. And come *straight* back.'

The van turns on to Peartree Gardens, tinkling 'Greensleeves'. Jimmy hurries towards it, rehearsing his story. *I had 'em, Mam: two ninety-nines with flakes and choc sauce and everything, then this dog dashes out and trips me up and I drop 'em.* That, plus a few tears, ought to do the trick.

He approaches the van, mouth dry with anticipation. Viv smiles out at him. 'Yes love, what can I get you?'

His answer masks the genie's gleeful laugh.